AF522382

The yellowbacks... classics of popular fiction

The yellowjackets or yellowbacks were a great series of bestselling adventure and crime thrillers that had its origins in the mid to late 19th century following on from the 'penny dreadfuls'. They virtually began the mass market revolution of the early 20th century with a clear standard format and imprint/series livery (what would today be called branding). Hodder & Stoughton published the yellowjackets in two main series with series run dates of: 1923-1939 and later 1949-1957.

As the tagline ('where thrillers really began') on the back cover implies, the imprint and series focused on thrillers that were the bestsellers of their time. This current reissue or retro revival if you will, brings back many of these masterpieces, now classics in their own way and extends it further by including key titles from that period that were either great crime or thriller or even general commercial fiction (including sub-genres of noir, horror, gothic, romance, westerns, etc.) influences of their time. There are some perennial favourites and many rarities either lost or not easily available being revived in the current series. Writers and characters ranged from adventure heroes like Bulldog Drummond, Allan Quatermain, Richard Hannay or the Saint through thriller grandmasters Edgar Wallace and E. Phillips Oppenheim, crime and mystery maestros like Patricia Wentworth, GK Chesterton, Agatha Christie and the Detection club, to western and swashbucklers like Zane Grey, Max Brand, Captain Blood and even romance or general fiction classics like Hermina Black, Denise Robins, Marie Corelli or Stella Morton. These were books that had storytelling at their heart and always entertained.

The yellowbacks had both hardback (with varying design elements) and paperback (which built the series look) versions with the latter still carrying the imprint 'yellowjacket'. The current reissues pay tribute to both and use an amalgam of elements from both editions while retaining the complete yellow (or 'mustard-plaster') livery with the author's name in blue beveled type with a 'simulated emboss' effect and a white outer 'outline', and the book title in black. These reissues retain the distinctive size of the original mass market paperback and follow the three main category variations—the thrillers (crime, westerns, mystery, adventure) had blue lettering for the author's name, while Romance and softer general fiction had red; and other categories like humour had green.

For more detail and a full list of titles visit https://www.hachetteindia.com/home/yellowbacks

DEVLIN THE BARBER

DEVLIN THE BARBER

Benjamin Leopold Farjeon (12 May 1838 – 23 July 1903) was an English novelist, playwright, printer and journalist. As an author, he was known for his huge output. Farjeon began writing novels and plays, as a self-confessed disciple of Dickens, whose attention he managed to catch. In his novel *Grif: A Story of Australian Life,* for example, he modelled the Melbourne Street Arab Grif on Jo in *Bleak House*. In 1868, he returned to Britain and lived in London in the Adelphi Theatre.

Over the next 35 years, Farjeon produced nearly 60 novels. Many of his works were illustrated by his long-time friend Nicholas Chevalier.

Benjamin Farjeon died in Hampstead on 23 July 1903, aged 65.

DEVLIN
THE BARBER

B. L. Farjeon

Devlin the Barber
First Published by Ward and Downey, London in 1888.

This Hodder Yellowback edition © Hachette India 2023
(Registered Name: Hachette Book Publishing India Pvt. Ltd.)
An Hachette UK Company www.hachetteindia.com

1

The texts in these editions in most cases have been reprinted as is, with minimal editorial changes and by and large no bowdlerizing for political correctness; though in some editions, a few words and phrases considered archaic, or those considered offensive now, along with archaic punctuation may have been modified in places to make the text more accessible to today's readers. The narratives, language, beliefs, social mores and/or cultural depictions, in these volumes are a reflection of their times and must be viewed as such. They may also contain certain cultural, racial and gender prejudices and stereotypes that may be outdated or clearly wrong then and wrong today; but their removal would be tantamount to claiming these prejudices never existed. The Publisher does not endorse or support those depictions or stereotypes; and these books have been made available for a discerning audience that will read it for entertainment value and a chronicle/record of popular fiction of past times.

Cover design by Priya Singh adapted from the original classic yellowjacket by Hodder & Stoughton.

Cover illustration by Ishan Trivedi.

Series note: Some of the books in the series (unless otherwise credited) may have cover or inside illustrations from the original yellowbacks or early editions, and while full restoration has been attempted, some images may be grainy or faded due to the condition of the original material. The end notes or bonus material or blurb details may have been sourced from the public domain or free use publications such as Wikipedia and attribution is hereby made also allowing similar free use reproduction from here. Sources requiring further specific attribution may write in and further detailing and/or corrections shall be made in subsequent printings/editions.

Reprint specifications may be subject to change including but not limited to finishes, paper, colour sections.

ISBN: 978-93-5731-036-9

Hachette Book Publishing India Pvt. Ltd.
4th & 5th Floors, Corporate Centre,
Plot No. 94, Sector 44, Gurugram - 122 003, India

Typeset in Electra LT STD 10/12.5 pt by Manipal Technologies Limited, Manipal

Printed and bound in India by Manipal Technologies Limited, Manipal

CONTENTS

Introduction	In which reference is made to a strange, unfathomable being, through whose instrumentality an awful mystery was solved	1
I.	In which an account is given of the good fortune which befell Mr. Melladew	3
II.	I am the recipient of terrible news	11
III.	A shoal of visitors – followed by another mystery	17
IV.	Mr. Richard Portland makes a singular proposition to me	25
V.	I pay a visit to Mrs. Lemon	32
VI.	I am haunted by three evil-looking objects in Mrs. Lemon's room	36
VII.	Devlin's first introduction into the mystery	44
VIII.	I make the acquaintance of George Carton's guardian, Mr. Kenneth Dowsett	49
IX.	Fanny Lemon relates under what circumstances she resolved to let her second floor front	57
X.	Devlin the Barber takes Fanny's first floor front	63
XI.	Devlin performs some wonderful tricks, fascinates Mr. Lemon, and strikes terror to the soul of Fanny Lemon	67
XII.	Fanny Lemon relates how her husband, after becoming better acquainted with Devlin the Barber, seemed to be haunted by shadows and spirits	74

XIII.	In which Fanny narrates how her husband had a fit, and what the doctor thought of it	83
XIV.	Devlin appears suddenly, and holds a conversation with Fanny about the murder	89
XV.	Fanny describes how she made up her mind what to do with Lemon	94
XVI.	Mr. Lemon wakes up	98
XVII.	Lemon's vision in the Twisted Cow	105
XVIII.	Fanny's story being concluded, I pay a visit to Mr. Lemon, and resolve to interview Devlin the Barber	110
XIX.	Face to face with Devlin, I demand an explanation of him	114
XX.	Devlin astonishes me	120
XXI.	Devlin and I make a compact	130
XXII.	I send Devlin's desk to my wife, and smoke a fragrant cigar	138
XXIII.	I pass a morning in Devlin's place of business	146
XXIV.	Mr. Kenneth Dowsett gives me the slip	155
XXV.	We follow in pursuit	163
XXVI.	Another strange and unexpected discovery	175
XXVII.	We track Mr. Kenneth Dowsett to Boulogne	182
XXVIII.	The trance and the revelation	191
XXIX.	The rescue	197
XXX.	Devlin's last scheme	202

Introduction

IN WHICH REFERENCE IS MADE TO A STRANGE, UNFATHOMABLE BEING THROUGH WHOSE INSTRUMENTALITY AN AWFUL MYSTERY WAS SOLVED

The manner in which I became intimately associated with a fearful mystery with which not only all London but all England was ringing, and the strange, inexplicable Being whom the course of events brought to my knowledge, are so startling and wonderful, that I have grown to believe that by no effort of the imagination, however wild and bewildering the labyrinths into which it may lead a man, can the actual realism of our everyday life be outrivalled. What I am about to narrate is absolutely true – somewhat of an unnecessary statement, for the reason that human fancy could never have invented it. To a person unfamiliar with the wondrous life of a great city like London the story may appear impossible, but there are thousands of men and women who will immediately recognise in it features with which they became acquainted through the columns of the newspapers. I venture to say that the leading incident by which one morning – it was but yesterday – the great city was thrilled and horrified can never be entirely effaced from their memories. Dark crimes and deeds of heroism, in which the incidents are pathetic or pitiful, draw even strangers into sympathetic relation with each other. These events come home to us, as it were. What happened to one whose face we have never seen, whose hand we have never grasped, may happen to us who move in the same familiar grooves of humanity. Our hopes and fears, our joys and sorrows, our duties and temptations, are the same, because we are human; and it is this common tie of kinship that will cause the story of Devlin the Barber to be received with more than ordinary interest. Now, for the first time is revealed, in these pages, the strange manner in which the fearful mystery in which it was enshrouded was unravelled. The facts are as I shall relate them, and whatever the impression they may create, a shuddering curiosity must inevitably be aroused as to the nature and movements of the inscrutable Being through whose instrumentality I was made the agent in revealing what would otherwise have remained for ever hidden from human knowledge. By a few incredulous persons – I refer to those to whom nothing spiritual is demonstrable – the existence of this Being may be doubted; but nonetheless does he live and move among us this very day, pursuing his mission with a purpose and to an end which it is not in the power of mortal insight to fathom. It is not unlikely that some of my readers may have come unconsciously in contact with him within the last few hours.

I

IN WHICH AN ACCOUNT IS GIVEN OF THE GOOD FORTUNE WHICH BEFELL MR. MELLADEW

I am a struggling man – the phrase will be well understood, for the class to which I belong is a large one – and I reside in a neighbourhood which is neither very poor nor very fashionable. I have, of course, my friends and acquaintances, and among the most intimate of the former is a family of the name of Melladew.

Mr. Melladew is a reader in a printing-office in which a weekly newspaper is printed. Mrs. Melladew, with the assistance of one small servant, manages the home. They had two daughters, twins, eighteen years of age, named respectively Mary and Elizabeth. These girls were very beautiful, and were so much alike that they were frequently mistaken for one another. Mrs. Melladew has told me that when they were very young she was compelled to make some distinguishing mark in their dress to avoid confusion in her recognition of them, such as differently coloured socks or pieces of ribbon. The home of the Melladews was a happy one, and the sisters loved each other sincerely. They were both in outdoor employment, in the establishments of a general linendraper and a fashionable dressmaker. Mary was in the employment of the linendraper – Limbird's, in Regent Street. It is a firm of wide repute, and employs a great number of hands, some of whom sleep in the house. This was the case with Mary Melladew, who went to her work on Monday morning and did not return home until Saturday night. Elizabeth, or Lizzie as she was always called, was employed by Madame Michel, in Baker Street. She went to her work at half-past eight every morning and returned home at half-past seven every night.

The printing-office in which Mr. Melladew is engaged employs two readers, a night reader and a day reader. Mr. Melladew is the day reader, his hours being from nine in the morning till seven in the evening. But on Saturdays he has a much longer spell; he is due in the office at eight in the morning, and he remains until two or three hours past midnight – a stretch of eighteen or nineteen hours. By that time all the work for the Sunday edition of the weekly newspaper is done, and the outside pages are being worked off on the steam presses.

Now, upon the Saturday morning on which, so far as I am concerned, the enthralling interest of my story commences, certain important events had occurred in my career and in that of Mr. Melladew. Exactly one month previous to that day, the firm in which I had been employed for a great many years had given me a month's notice to leave. My dismissal was not caused by any lapse of duty on my part; it was simply that business had been for some time in a bad state, and that my employers found it necessary to reduce their staff. Among those who received notice to quit, I, unfortunately, was included. Therefore, when I rose on Saturday morning I was in the dismal position of a man out of work, my time having expired on the day before. This was of serious importance to me. With Mr. Melladew the case was different. In what unexpectedly occurred to him there was bright sunshine, to be succeeded by black darkness.

He had visited me on the Friday night, and I perceived at once that he was in a state of intense and pleasurable excitement.

"I have come to tell you some good news," he said.

For a moment I thought that this good news might affect myself, and might bring about a favourable turn in my affairs, but Mr. Melladew's next words dispelled the hope.

"I am the happiest man in London," he said.

I reflected gravely, but not enviously, upon my own position, and waited for Mr. Melladew to explain himself.

"Did I ever mention to you," he asked, "that I had a brother-in-law in Australia?"

"Yes," I replied, "you have spoken of him lately two or three times."

"So many years had passed," said Mr. Melladew, "since my wife heard from him that I had almost forgotten him. He is her brother, you know, and his name is Portland – Richard Portland. That was my wife's name before we were married – not Richard, of course, but Portland." He laughed, and rubbed his leg with his right hand; in his left hand was a letter. "It was about eight months ago that we received a letter from him, asking us to give him information about our family and circumstances. He did not say anything about his own, so we were left quite in the dark as to whether he was rich or poor, or a married man or a bachelor. However, my wife answered his letter, and sent him the pictures of our two girls, and in her letter she asked whether he was married and had a family, and said also that she would like him to send us their pictures. Well, we heard nothing further from him till today. Another letter came from him while I was at the office. You may read it; there is nothing private in it. It isn't from Australia; it is written from Southampton, you see. But that is not the only surprise in it."

I took the letter and read it. It was, indeed, a letter to give pleasurable surprise to the receiver. Without any announcement to Mr. Melladew of his intention, Mr. Portland had left Australia, and was now in Southampton. He intended to start by an early train on Saturday morning for London, and would come straight to his brother-in-law's house. In the letter he replied to the questions put by Mrs. Melladew. He was a bachelor, without family ties of any kind in Australia. Moreover, he had made his fortune, and it was the portraits of his two nieces which were the main cause of his return to England. Their beauty had evidently made a deep impression upon him. He spoke of them and of Mrs. Melladew in the most affectionate terms, and said it was a great pleasure to him to think that he was coming to a home which he hoped he might look upon as partly his own. He sent his warmest love to them all, and in pleasantly tender words, the meaning of which could scarcely be mistaken, he desired a message to be given to his "dear nieces," to the effect that "their ship had come home." I handed the letter back to Mr. Melladew, and expressed my gratification at the good news.

"It is good news," he said gleefully, "the best of news. I knew you would be pleased. I am wondering whether it is a large or a small fortune he has made. My wife says a large one."

"And *I* say a large one," I remarked.

"What makes you of that opinion?" inquired Mr. Melladew.

"Well, in the first place there are so many large fortunes made in Australia."

"That is true."

"Then, money being so much more plentiful there than here, a man gets to think less of a little than we do. His ideas become larger, I mean. At any time these last dozen years a hundred pounds would have been a Godsend to me, and I should have thought of it so—"

"So would I," interposed Mr. Melladew.

"But if you and I were in a land of gold, we should, I daresay, think much more lightly of a hundred pounds. I wish I had emigrated when I was first married; I had the chance, and let it slip. But it's no use crying over spilt milk."

"Not a bit of use," said Mr. Melladew; "life's a perpetual grind here, and I am truly grateful for the light this letter has let in upon us. You've given me two reasons for thinking my brother-in-law's fortune a large one. Have you any others?"

"Well, he speaks of your daughters' ship having come home. That looks as if he meant to provide for them."

"It *does* look like it," said Mr. Melladew; and I saw that my arguments had given him pleasure. "My wife has a reason, also, for thinking so. She says, when Dick – that is her brother, you know – went away he declared he would never come back to England unless he could come back a very rich man. 'And,' says my wife, 'what Dick said, he'd stick to.' She is sure of that. It's wonderful, isn't it? He didn't have a sovereign to bless himself with when he left England, and now – but it's no use speculating. We shall know everything soon. You will understand my feelings; you have children of your own."

I had indeed, and it made me rueful to think of them. Getting another situation in such hard times was no easy matter.

"It isn't for myself," resumed Mr. Melladew, "that I am overjoyed at the better prospect before us: it is for my girls. Perhaps it means that they will not have to go out to work any longer. They are good girls, but they are so pretty, and have such engaging ways, that I have often been disturbed by the circumstance of their not being so much under my own and their mother's eyes as we would wish them to be. It could not be helped hitherto. There's the question of dress, now. You can manage tolerably well when they're little girls; a clever woman like my wife can turn and twist, and cut up old things in a way to make the little ones look quite nice; but when they become young women, with all sorts of new ideas in their pretty heads, it is another pair of shoes. It's natural, too, that they should want a little pocket money to spend upon innocent pleasures and harmless vanities. We were young ourselves once, weren't we? We found we couldn't afford to give the girls what they wanted. They saw it, too, so they made up their minds, without saying a word to us, to look out for situations for themselves, and for months they haven't been a farthing's expense to us. They even give their mother a trifle a week towards the home. Good girls, the best of girls; I should be a miserable man without them. Still, as I said, I have been uneasy about them: there are so many scoundrels in the world ready with honeyed words to turn a girl's head; and it hurts me to think that they have their little secrets which they don't ask us to share. Now, thank God, it will be all right. My brother-in-law will be here tomorrow, and when he sees Lizzie and Mary he will be confirmed in his kind intentions towards them. They can leave their situations; and if any man wishes to pay them attentions he can do so in a straightforward manner in the home in which they were brought up."

He was in the blithest of spirits, and I cordially renewed my congratulations on his good fortune. In return, he condoled with me on the unpromising change in my own prospects. I was not very cheerful – no man could be in such a position – but I am not in the habit of magnifying my misfortunes to my friends, and I plucked up my spirits.

"You will soon get another situation," said Mr. Melladew.

"I hope so," I replied; "I cannot afford to keep long out of one."

"It may be in my power to give you a lift," he said kindly. "Who knows what may turn up in the course of the next few hours?"

I attached no signification to this not uncommon remark at the time it was uttered, but it recurred to me afterwards, charged with sad and terrible import. We fell to again discussing the matter of which he was full.

"I am almost ashamed of my good luck," said Mr. Melladew, "when I think what has happened to you."

"A man must accept the ups and downs of life with courage," I said, "and must put the best face he can upon them."

We were true friends, and I had a sincere respect for him as a worthy fellow who had faithfully performed his duties to his family and employers. He was passionately fond of his two daughters, and frequently spoke of them as the greatest blessing in his life. It was, indeed, delightful to witness the affection he bestowed upon them in the happy home of which he was the head. They were girls of which any man might have been proud, being not only beautiful, but bright and witty, and full of animation.

Mr. Melladew and I chatted together for another half-hour, and then he wished me goodnight.

"It is fortunate," he said, "that I got away from the office an hour earlier than usual. I shall be at home when Lizzie returns from her work, and I want to be the first to tell her the good news. How excited she will be! There was a friend at the house last night, who told us our fortunes. Lizzie is very fond of having her fortune told. 'There, father,' she says, 'didn't my fortune say that I was to receive a letter? And I've got one.' As if there was anything out of the way in receiving a letter! Last night she was told that a great and wonderful surprise was in store for her. Well, there is, but I am certain the fortuneteller knew as much about its nature as the man in the moon."

"And Mary?" I said. "Will you tell her tonight?"

"No," replied Mr. Melladew, "we will wait till she comes home tomorrow. When she sees her uncle from Australia sitting in my armchair, she won't know what to think of it. Happy girls, happy girls!"

"And happy father and mother, too," I said.

"Yes, yes," he said, with great feeling, "and happy father and mother too."

It was in no envious spirit that I contrasted his good luck with my bad, but had I suspected what the next few hours had in store for him, I should have thanked God for my lot. We have reason to be profoundly grateful for the ills we escape.

II

I AM THE RECIPIENT OF TERRIBLE NEWS

On Saturday morning I rose early, with the strange feelings of a man whose habits of life had been suddenly and violently wrenched out of their usual course. I wandered up and down the stairs and into all the rooms in the house, and to the street-door, where I stood looking vacantly along the street, perhaps for the situation I had lost, as though it were something I had dropped by accident and could pick up again. Two or three neighbours passed and gave me good-morning, and one paused and asked if I was not well.

"Not well?" I echoed, somewhat irritably; "I am well, quite well. What makes you think otherwise?"

"O," he answered apologetically, "only seeing you here, that's all. It's so unusual."

He passed on, looking once or twice behind him. Unusual? Of course it was unusual. Everything was unusual, everything in the world, which seemed to be turned topsy-turvy. If the people in the street had walked on their heads instead of their feet it would not have surprised me very much. I should have regarded it as quite in keeping with the fact that I was standing at my own street-door in idleness at half-past eight o'clock on a Saturday morning; I could not remember the time when such a thing had occurred to me.

Standing thus in a state of semi-stupefaction, the postman came up and gave me a letter. This recalled me to myself.

"Now," thought I, as I turned the envelope over in my hand, 'whom is it from, and what does it contain?"

At first I had an unreasonable hope that it was from my employers, imploring me to come back, but a glance at the address convinced me that it was a foolish hope. The writing was strange to me, and the envelope was a common one, and was fastened with sealing-wax bearing the impression of a thimble. I opened and read the letter, and although it did not contain the offer of a situation, or hold out the prospect of one, the contents interested me. I shall have occasion presently to refer to this letter more particularly, and shall at present content myself with saying that had it not arrived this story would never have been written. While my wife and I were at breakfast we spoke of it, and I said it was my intention to comply with the request it contained.

Over breakfast, also, we reviewed our position. During my years of employment I had managed to save very little money, and upon reckoning up what I had in my purse and what I owed, I arrived at a balance in my favour of a little less than four pounds, which represented the whole of my worldly wealth. A poor lookout, and I was reflecting upon it gloomily, when my good little wife, with a tender deprecatory smile, laid before me on the table a Post Office savings-book.

"What is this?" I asked.

"Look," she replied.

The book was made out in her name, and the small deposits, extending over a number of years, made therein showed a credit of more than twenty pounds.

"Yours?" I said, in wonder. "Really yours?"

"No," said my wife. "Yours."

My heart beat with joy; these twenty pounds were like a reprieve. I should have time to look about, without being tortured by fears of immediate want. I drew my wife to my side, and embraced her. Twenty pounds, with which to commence over again the battle of life! Why it was a fortune! How the little woman had contrived to save so much out of her scanty housekeeping money was a mystery to me, but she had done it by hook or by crook, as the saying is, and she now experienced a true and sweet delight in handing it over to me.

"Well," said I, rubbing my hands cheerfully, "things might look worse than they do – a great deal worse. We have a little store to help us over compulsorily idle days, and, thank God, all the children are well."

It was much to be grateful for, and we kissed each other in token of our gratitude, and also as a pledge that we would not lose heart, but would battle bravely on.

I had just finished my second cup of tea when the street-door was hastily opened, and my friend Mr. Melladew staggered, or rather fell, into the room, with a face as white as a ghost. His limbs were trembling so that he could not stand, and my wife, much alarmed, started up and helped him into a chair.

On this special morning we had breakfasted late, and as my wife was assisting Mr. Melladew the clock struck ten.

It sometimes happens that the most ordinary occurrences become of unusual importance by reason of circumstances with which they have no connection. Thus it was that the striking of ten o'clock, as I gazed upon the white face of my visitor, filled me with an apprehension of impending evil.

"Good God!" I cried. "What has happened?" My thought was that there had been an accident to the train by which Mr. Melladew expected his brother-in-law from Southampton, but I was soon undeceived. It was difficult to extract anything intelligible from Mr. Melladew in his terrible state of agitation; but eventually I was placed in possession of the following particulars.

Mr. Melladew had risen early and had left his wife abed, and, as he supposed, his daughter Lizzie. It was Mrs. Melladew's custom on Saturday mornings to take half-an-hour extra in the way of sleep, and Mr. Melladew would prepare his own breakfast on these occasions. He did so on this morning, and left his house at twenty minutes to eight. At eight o'clock punctually he was sitting at his desk in the printing-office, reading proofs. Everything was going on as usual, the only pleasant difference being the extraordinary lightness of Mr. Melladew's heart as he thought of his rich brother-in-law from Australia, perhaps at that very hour stepping into the train for London, and of his two darling children, Lizzie and Mary. He did not, however, allow this contemplation to interfere with the faithful and steady discharge of his duties, and his work proceeded uninterruptedly until half-past nine, when he sent his young assistant, a reading boy, into the composing-room with the last proofs he had read, telling him to bring back any more that were ready. A workman at the galley-press had just pulled off a column of newly set-up matter, and the lad, without waiting for it to be delivered to him, took the slip from the printer's hand, and returned quickly to the reading-room. Mr. Melladew, receiving the slip from his assistant, was about to commence arranging the "copy," which the lad had also brought with him, when a compositor rushed in, and, snatching both slip and "copy' from Mr. Melladew's desk, hurriedly left the room.

"What's that for?" inquired Mr. Melladew.

"I don't know, sir," replied the lad; "but there's something 'up' in the composing-room. The men are all standing talking in a regular fluster."

"What about?"

"Ain't got a notion, sir; but they seem regular upset."

Curious to ascertain what was going on, Mr. Melladew strolled into the composing-room, and was struck by the sudden silence which ensued upon his entrance. It was all the more singular because Mr. Melladew, as he pushed the door open, heard the men speaking in excited voices, and had half a fancy that he heard his own name uttered in tones of pity. "Poor Melladew!" Yes, it was not a fancy. The words had been uttered at the moment of his entrance. The silence of the compositors, their pitying looks, confirmed it. But why should they speak of him as "poor Melladew" at a time when life had never been so bright and fair? What was the meaning of the pitying glances directed towards him? The composing-room, especially on Saturdays, was a scene of lively bustle and animation, but now the men were standing idle, stick in hand, at the corners of their frames, or tiptoeing over their cases, and the eyes of every man there were fixed upon Mr. Melladew. Had he been in trouble, had his wife or one of his darling daughters been ill, his thoughts would have immediately flown to his home, and he would have seen in the pitying glances of the compositors a sign of some dread misfortune; but in his happy mood he received no such impression.

"What on earth is the matter with you all?" he said in a light tone.

He saw the compositor who had snatched the slip of new matter from his desk, and before he could be prevented he took it from the man's hand.

The compositors found their voices.

"No, Mr. Melladew!" they cried. "No; don't, don't!"

"Nonsense!" he said, and keeping possession of the slip, he left the composing-room for his own.

"Go and get the copy," he said to the lad who had followed him.

When the lad was gone he spread the slip on the desk before him. The first words he saw formed the title of the column he was about to read: "Horrible Murder in Victoria Park!" Beneath it were the sub-headings, "Stabbed to the Heart!" and "A Bunch of Blood-stained Daisies!" To a newspaper reader such events, shocking though they be, are unhappily no novelties, and Mr. Melladew looked down the column, I will not say mechanically, for he was a humane man, but steadily, and stirred no doubt by pity and indignation. But before he had got halfway down the pulsations of his heart seemed to stop, and the words swam before his eyes. His eyes lighted on the name of the girl who had been murdered.

It was that of his own daughter, Lizzie Melladew!

III

A SHOAL OF VISITORS FOLLOWED BY ANOTHER MYSTERY

In an agony of horror and despair he had flown from the printing-office to my house.

I cannot say whether he chose my house premeditatedly; it is likely that it was done without distinct intention, but it was a proof that he regarded my friendship as genuine, and that he knew he could depend upon my sympathy in times of trouble. As indeed he could. My heart bled as I gazed upon him. The words issued with difficulty from his trembling lips; his features were convulsed; he shook like a man in an ague.

"O, my Lizzie!" he moaned. "My poor, poor Lizzie! O, my child, my child!"

I took in regularly a penny daily newspaper, and I had read it on this morning, but there was no mention in its columns of the dreadful occurrence. The discovery had been made too late for the first editions of the daily journals.

Mr. Melladew's story being told, disjointedly, and in fragments which I had to piece together in order to arrive at an intelligible comprehension of it, the unhappy man sat before me, moaning.

"O, my Lizzie! O, my poor child!"

"Was she at home?" I asked gently; I did not attempt to console him. Of what avail were mere words at such a moment? "Was she at home when you went from here last night?" "

"Yes, she was there," he moaned. "When she went to bed I kissed her. For the last time! For the last, last time!"

And then he broke down utterly. I could get nothing further from him.

When she went to bed, he kissed her. What kind of riddle was here, in the midst of the horrible tragedy, that the hapless girl should have wished her parents goodnight and retired to rest, and be found ruthlessly murdered a few hours afterwards in an open park at some distance from her house? With such joyful news as Mr. Melladew had to communicate to his daughter, the probability was that they had kept up later than usual, talking of the brighter future that then seemed spread before them. It made the tragic riddle all the more difficult.

There came a knock at the street-door, and a gentleman was admitted, upon most urgent business he said. It turned out that he was a newspaper reporter, who, in advance of the police, had tracked Mr. Melladew to my house, and had come to obtain information from him for his newspaper. I pointed out to him the condition of Mr. Melladew, and said something to the effect that it was scarcely decent to intrude upon him at such a time.

The reporter, who evidently felt deeply for the bereaved father, and whose considerate manner was such as to completely disarm me, said aside to me,

"Pray do not think that I am devoid of feeling; I am a father myself, and have a daughter of the age of his poor girl. My mission is not one of idle curiosity. A ruthless murder has been committed, and the murderer is at large. I am not working only for my paper; I am assisting the cause of justice. Every scrap of information we can obtain will hasten the arrest of the wretch who has been guilty of a crime so diabolical."

"He can tell you nothing," I said, compelled to admit that he was right. "Look at him as he sits there, crushed and broken down by the blow."

"I pity him from my heart," said the reporter. "Can you assist me in any way? Did the poor girl live at home?"

"She lived at home certainly, but she had employment at Madame Michel's, in Baker Street."

"Madame Michel's, in Baker Street. I must go there. Did she sleep out?"

"No; she came home every night at half-past seven."

"Did she do so last night?"

"Yes."

"Did she not go to some place of amusement?"

"Not to my knowledge. Her father told me that before she went to bed he kissed her goodnight."

"Do you know at what hour?"

"I do not"

"But presumably not early."

"Not so early as usual, I should say, because her father had some good news to communicate to her, and they would stop up late talking of it. Understand, much of what I say is presumptive."

"But reasonable," said the reporter. "Did the poor girl have a sweetheart?"

Words which Mr. Melladew had spoken on the previous night recurred to me here. "There are so many scoundrels in the world ready with honeyed words to turn a girl's head; and it hurts me to think that they have their little secrets which they don't ask us to share." Did not this point to a secret which was hidden from her parents? I said nothing of this to the reporter, but answered that I was not aware that the poor girl had a sweetheart.

"Someone must have been in love with her," said the reporter.

"Many, perhaps," I rejoined; "but not one courted her openly, I believe – that is, to her parents' knowledge."

"That counts for very little. She was a beautiful girl."

"How?" I exclaimed. "Have you seen her?"

"I saw her this morning," he answered gravely, "within the last two hours. She looked like an angel."

"Was there no trace of suffering in her face?" I asked wistfully.

"None. She was stabbed to the heart – only one, sharp, swift, devilish blow, and death must have been instantaneous. To my unprofessional eye it almost seems as if she must have died in sleep – in happy sleep."

"That, at least, is merciful. Hush!"

Mr. Melladew was rocking to and fro murmuring, "O, my Lizzie, my darling child! O, my poor, poor Lizzie!" We had spoken in low tones, and he evinced no consciousness of having heard what we said. During our conversation the reporter was jotting down notes unobtrusively. The conversation would doubtless have been continued had it not been for the appearance of other persons, following rapidly upon each other, policemen, and additional reporters, who had discovered that Mr. Melladew was in my house. The last to appear was Mrs. Melladew, who had heard rumours of the frightful crime, and who flew round to me, not knowing that her husband was in the room. What passed from that moment, while all these persons were buzzing around me, was so confusing that I cannot hope to give an intelligible transcript of it. I was, as it were, in the background, as one who had no immediate interest in the unravelling of the terrible mystery. It was a most agitating time to me and my wife, and when my visitors had all departed I felt like a man who had been afflicted by a horrible nightmare. How little did I imagine that the letter I had received by the early morning's post, and which I had in my pocket, was vitally connected with it, and that of all those present I was the man who was destined to bring the mystery to light!

Before the day was over fresh surprises were in store for me in connection with the dreadful deed. Needless to say that the whole neighbourhood was in a state of great excitement; so numerous were my idle visitors that I was compelled to tell my wife to admit into the house no person but the Melladews, or relatives of theirs. In the afternoon, however, one visitor called who would not be denied. He sent in his card, which bore the name of George Carton, and I said I would see him.

He was a young man, whose age I judged to be between twenty and twenty-five, well dressed, and remarkably good-looking. His manners were those of one who was accustomed to move in good society, and both his speech and behaviour during the interview impressed me favourably. I observed when he entered the room that he was greatly agitated.

"I have intruded myself upon you, sir," he said, "because I felt that I should go mad if I did not speak to some person who was a friend of – or—"

He could not proceed, and I finished the sentence for him. "Of the poor girl who has been so cruelly murdered?"

He nodded his head, and, when he could control his voice, said, "You were an intimate friend of hers, sir?"

"Mr. Melladew's family and mine," I replied, "have been on terms of friendship for many years. I have known the poor girl and her sister since their infancy."

"I did not dare to call upon Mr. Melladew," he said, and then he faltered again and paused.

"Are you acquainted with him?" I asked.

"No," he said, "but I hoped to be. If I went now and told him what I wish to impart to you, he might look upon me as responsible for what has occurred." He put his hand over his eyes, from which the tears were flowing.

"What is it you wish to impart to me?" I inquired, "and why should you suppose you would be held responsible for so horrible a crime?"

"I scarcely know what I am saying," he replied. "But my secret intimacy with Lizzie" – I caught my breath at his familiar utterance of the name – "becoming known to him now for the first time, might put wrong ideas into his head."

"Your secret intimacy with Lizzie?" I exclaimed.

"We have known each other for more than four months," he said.

"Secretly?"

"Yes, secretly."

"And the poor girl's parents were not aware of it?"

"They were not. It was partly my poor Lizzie's wish, and partly my own, I think, until I was sure that I possessed her love. She kept it from me for a long time. 'Wait,' she used to say, smiling – pardon me, sir; my heart seems as if it would break when I speak of her – 'Wait,' she used to say, 'I am not certain yet whether I really, really love you.' But she did, sir, all along."

"How do you know that?" I asked, in doubt now whether I should regard him with favour or suspicion.

"She confessed it to me last Tuesday night as she walked home from Baker Street."

"You were in the habit of meeting her, then?"

"Yes. I beg you to believe, sir, there was nothing wrong in it. I loved and honoured her sincerely. I wanted then to accompany her home and ask her parents' permission to pay my addresses to her openly: but she said no, and that she would speak to them first herself. It was arranged so. She was to tell them tonight, and I was to call and see her father and mother tomorrow. And now – and now –" Again he paused, overpowered by grief. Presently he spoke again. "See here, sir."

He detached a locket from his chain, and opening it, showed me the sweet and beautiful face of Lizzie Melladew.

"It was taken for me," he said, "on Wednesday morning. She obtained permission from her employers for an hour's absence, and we went together to get it taken. The photographer hurried the picture on for me, I was so anxious for it. I had my picture taken for her, and put into a locket, which I was to give her tomorrow with this ring in the presence of her parents." He produced both the locket and the ring. The locket was a handsome gold ornament, set with pearls; the ring was a half-hoop, set with diamonds. The gifts were such as only a man in a good position could afford to give. "I shall never be happy again," he said mournfully, as he replaced the locket on his chain, after gazing on the beautiful face with eyes of pitiful love.

"Were you in the habit of writing to her?" I asked.

"No, sir. No letters passed between us; there was no need to write, I saw her so often – four or five times a week. 'When father and mother know everything,' she said on Tuesday night, 'you shall write to me every day.' I promised that I would."

"I am not sorry you confided in me," I said, completely won over by the young man's ingenuousness and undoubted sincerity; "but I can offer you no words of comfort. You will have to make this known to others."

"I shall do what is right, sir. It is not in your power, nor in any man's, to give me any comfort or consolation. The happiness of my life is destroyed – but there is still one thing left me, and I will not rest till it is accomplished. As God is my judge, I will not!" He did not give me time to ask his meaning, but continued: "You can do me the greatest favour, sir."

"What is it?"

"I must see Mary – her sister, sir. Can you send round to the house, and ask her to come and see me here? She *will* come when she gets my message. Will you do this for me, sir?"

"Yes," I replied, "there is no harm in it."

I called my wife, and bade her go to Mr. Melladew's house, and contrive to see Mary Melladew privately, and give her the young man's message. During my wife's absence George Carton and I exchanged but few words. He sat for the chief part of the time with his head resting on his hand, and I was busy thinking whether the information he had imparted to me would be likely to afford a clue to the discovery of the murderer. My wife returned with consternation depicted on her face.

"Mary is not at home," she said.

"Where has she gone?" cried George Carton, starting up.

To my astonishment my wife replied, "They are in the greatest trouble about her. She has not been home all the day."

"Have they not seen anything of her?" I asked, also rising to my feet.

"No," said my wife, "they have seen nothing whatever of her."

"Is it possible," I exclaimed, "that she can be still at her place of business, in ignorance of what has taken place?"

"No," cried George Carton, in great excitement, "she is not there. I have been to inquire. She went out last night, and never returned. Great God! What can be the meaning of it?"

I strove in vain to calm him. He paced the room with flashing eyes, muttering to himself words so wild that I could not arrive at the least understanding of them.

"Gone! Gone!" he cried at last. "But where, where? I will not sleep, I will not rest, till I find her! Neither will I rest till I discover the murderer of my darling girl! And when I discover him, when he stands before me, as there is a living God, I will kill him with my own hands!"

His passion was so intense that I feared he would there and then commit some act of violence, and I made an endeavour to restrain and calm him by throwing my arms around him; but he broke from me with a torrent of frantic words, and rushed out of the house.

Here was another mystery, added to the tragedy of the last few hours. What was to be the outcome of it? From what quarter was light to come?

IV

MR. RICHARD PORTLAND MAKES A SINGULAR PROPOSITION TO ME

In the evening I received another visitor, in the person of Mr. Richard Portland, Mr. Melladew's brother-in-law. A shrewd, hard-headed man, but much cast down at present. It was clear to me, after a little conversation with him, that his nieces, Mary and the hapless Lizzie, had been the great inducement of his coming home to England, and I learnt from him that there was no doubt about the news of Mary Melladew's mysterious disappearance.

Mr. Portland was a thoroughly practical man, even in matters of sentiment. It was sentiment truly that had brought him home, but his expectations had been blasted by the news of the tragedy which had greeted him on his arrival. He was deeply moved by the affliction which had fallen upon his sister's family; his indignation was aroused against the monster who had brought this fearful blow upon them; and, in addition, he was bitterly angry at being deprived of the society of two lovely, interesting girls, in whose hearts he had naturally hoped to find a place.

"My brother is fit for nothing," he said. "He is prostrate, and cannot be roused to action. He moans and moans, and clasps his head. My sister is no better; she goes out of one fainting fit into another."

"What can they do?" I asked. "What would you have them do?"

"Not sit idly down," he replied curtly. "That is not the way to discover the murderer; and discovered he must and shall be, if it costs me my fortune."

"There have been murders," I remarked, "in the very heart of London, and though years have passed, the murderers still walk the streets undetected."

"It is incredible," he said.

"It is true," was my rejoinder.

"But surely," he urged, "this will not be classed among them?"

"I trust not."

"Money will do much."

"Much, but not everything. You have been many years in Australia. Have not such crimes been committed even there without the perpetrators being brought to justice?"

"Yes," he replied, "but Australia and London are not to be spoken of in the same breath. There, a man may succeed in making himself lost in wild and vast tracts of country. He can walk for days without meeting a living soul. Here he is surrounded by his fellow creatures."

"Your argument," I said, "tells against yourself. Here, in the crush and turmoil of millions, each atom with its own individual and overwhelming cares and anxieties, the murderer is comparatively safe. No one notices him. Why should they, in such a seething crowd? In the bush he is the central figure; he walks along with a hang-dog look; he *must* halt at certain places for food, and his guilty manner draws attention upon him. In that lies his danger. But this is profitless argument. For my part, I see no reason why the murderer of your unfortunate niece should not be discovered."

"Sensibly said. It must be a man who committed the deed."

"That has to be proved," I remarked.

"Surely you don't believe it was a woman?" exclaimed Mr. Portland.

"Such things have been. In these cases of mystery it is always an error to rush at a conclusion and to set to work upon it, to the exclusion of all others. It is as great an error to reject a theory because of its improbability. My dear sir, nothing is improbable in this city of ours; I am almost tempted to say that nothing is impossible. The columns of our newspapers teem with romance which once upon a time would have been regarded as fables."

Mr. Portland looked at me thoughtfully as he said, "You are doubtless right. It needs such a mind as yours to bring the matter to light – a mind both comprehensive and microscopic. There is some satisfaction in speaking to you; a man hears things worth listening to. The unpractical stuff that has been buzzing in my ears ever since I arrived from Southampton has almost driven me crazy. Give me your careful attention for a few moments; it may be something in your pocket."

He paused awhile, as though considering a point, before he resumed.

"My coming home to the old country has been a bitter disappointment to me. Quite apart from the sympathy I feel for the parents upon whom such a dreadful blow has fallen, the news which greeted me on my arrival has upset the plans I had formed. Over there" – with a jerk of his thumb over his right shoulder, as though Australia lay immediately in the rear of his chair—"where I made a pretty considerable fortune, I had no family ties, and was often chewing the cud of loneliness, lamenting that I had no one to care for, and no one to care for me. When I received the portraits of my nieces I was captivated by them, and I thought of them continually. Here was the very thing I was sighing for, a human tie to banish the devil of loneliness from my heart. The beautiful young girls belonged to me in a measure, and would welcome and love me. I should have a home to go to where I should be greeted with affection. I won't dwell upon what I thought, because I hate a man who spins a thing out threadbare, but you will understand it. I came home to enjoy the society of my two beautiful nieces, and I find what you know of. Well, one poor girl has gone, and cannot be recalled; but the other, Mary, so far as we know, is alive; and yet she, too, disappeared last night, and nothing has been heard of her. She must be found; if she is in danger she must be rescued; she must be restored to her parents' arms, and to mine. Something else. The murderer of my poor niece Lizzie must be discovered and brought to justice – must be, I say! There shall be no miscarriage here; the villain shall not escape. Now, you – excuse me if I speak abruptly, I mean no disrespect by it; it is only my way of speaking; and I don't wish to be rude or to pry into your private affairs, far from it. What I mean is, money?"

I stared at him in amazement; he had stated his meaning in one pregnant word, but he had failed in conveying to my mind any comprehension of it.

"Now, I put it to you," he said, "and I hope you'll take it kindly. I give you my word that my intentions are good. You are not a rich man, are you?"

"No," I answered promptly; for he was so frank and open, and was speaking in a tone of such deep concern, that I could not take offence at a question which at other times I should have resented. "I am not."

"And you wouldn't turn your nose up at a thousand pounds?"

"No, indeed I would not," I said heartily, wondering what on earth the rich Australian was driving at.

"Well, then," he said, touching my breast with his forefinger, "you discover the murderer of my poor niece Lizzie, and the thousand pounds are yours. I will give the money to you.

Something else: find my niece Mary, and restore her to her parents and to me, and I'll make it two thousand. Come, you don't have such a chance every day."

"That is true," I said, and I could not help liking the old fellow for this display of heart. "But it is too remote for consideration."

"Not at all, my dear sir, not at all," and again he touched my breast with his forefinger; "there is nothing remote in it."

"But why," I asked, not at all convinced by his insistence, "do you offer *me* such a reward, instead of going to the police?"

"Partly because of what you said, confirmed – though I didn't think of it at the time you mentioned it – by what I have read, about murders being committed in the very heart of London, without the murderers ever being discovered."

"I was simply stating a fact."

"Exactly; and it speaks well for the police, doesn't it? But I have only explained part of my reason for offering you the reward. It isn't alone what you said about undiscovered murderers, it is because you spoke like a sensible man, who, once having his finger on a clue, wouldn't let it slip till he'd worked it right out; and like a man who, while he was working that clue, wouldn't let others slip that might happen to come in his way. I've opened my mind to you, and I've nothing more to say until you come to me to say something on your own account. O, yes I have, though; I was forgetting that we're strangers to one another, and that it wouldn't be reasonable for me to expect you to take my word for a thousand pounds. Well, then, to show you that I am in earnest, I lay on the table Bank of England notes for a hundred pounds. Here they are, on account."

To my astonishment he had pulled out his pocketbook and extracted ten ten-pound notes, and there they lay on the table before me. I would have entreated him to take them back, feeling that it would be the falsest of false pretences to accept them, but before I could speak again he was gone.

I called my wife into the room, and told her what had passed. She regarded it in the same light as myself, but I noted a little wistful look in her eyes as she glanced at the banknotes.

"A thousand pounds!" she sighed, half-longingly, half-humorously. "If we could only call it ours! Why, it would make our fortune!"

"It would, my dear," I said, wishing in my heart of hearts that I had a thousand pounds of my own to throw into her lap. "But this particular thousand pounds which the good old fellow has so generously offered will never come into our possession. So let us dismiss it from our minds."

"Mr. Portland," said my wife, "evidently thinks you would make a good detective."

"That may or may not be, though his opinion of me is altogether too flattering. Certainly, if I had a clue to the discovery of this terrible mystery – "

"You would follow it up," said my wife, finishing the sentence for me.

"Undoubtedly I would, with courage and determination. With such a reward in view, nothing should shake me off. I would prove myself a very bloodhound. But there," I said, half ashamed at being led away, "I am sailing in the clouds. Let's talk no more about it. As for Mr. Portland's hundred pounds I will put the notes carefully by, and return them to him at the first opportunity. Poor Mrs. Melladew! How I pity her and Melladew! I shall never forget the picture of the father sitting in that chair, moaning, 'My poor, poor Lizzie! O, my child, my child!' It was heartbreaking."

My wife and I talked a great deal of it during the night, and before we went to bed I had purchased at least seven or eight newspapers of the newsboys who passed through the street crying out new editions and latest news of the dreadful deed. But there was nothing really new. Matters were in the same state as when the body of the hapless girl was found in Victoria

Park early in the morning. I recognised how dangerous was the delay. Every additional hour increased the chances of the murderer's escape from the hands of justice.

I did not sleep well; my slumbers were disturbed by fantastic, horrible dreams. It was eleven o'clock on Sunday morning before I quitted my bed.

V

I PAY A VISIT TO MRS. LEMON

I must now speak of the letter which I received on the morning of the murder, as I stood at my street-door. It was from a Mrs. Lemon, entreating me to call upon her at any hour most convenient to me on this Sunday, and it was couched in terms so imploring that it would have been cruel on my part to refuse, more especially as the writer had some slight claim upon me. Mrs. Lemon had been for many years a nurse and servant in my parents' house, and the children were fond of her. She was then a spinster, and her name was Fanny Peel. We used to make jokes upon it, and call her Fancy Peel, Orange Peel, Candied Peel, Lemon Peel – and we little dreamt, when we called her Lemon Peel, that we were unconsciously moved by the spirit of prophecy. For though she was thirty years of age she succeeded in captivating a widower a few years older than herself, Ephraim Lemon, a master barber and hairdresser, who used to haunt the area. We youngsters were in the habit of watching for him and playing him tricks, I am afraid, but nothing daunted his ardour. He proposed for Fanny, and she accepted him. Some enterprising tradesmen, when their stock is stale or old-fashioned, put bills in their windows announcing that no reasonable offer will be refused. Fanny Peel, having been long on the shelf, may have thought of this when she accepted Ephraim Lemon's hand. After her marriage she came to see me once a year to pay her respects; but suddenly her visits became less frequent, until they ceased altogether. For a long time past I had heard nothing of my old nurse.

"It is a fine morning," I said to my wife, "and I shall walk to Fanny's house."

In the course of an hour I presented myself at Mrs. Lemon's street-door, and knocked. She herself opened it to me, and after an anxious scrutiny asked me eagerly to walk in. There was trouble in her face, tempered by an expression of relief when she fully recognised me. She preceded me into her little parlour, and I sat down, awaiting the communication she desired to make. Up to the point of my sitting down the only words exchanged between us were –

From her: "O, sir, it *is* you, and you *have* come!"

From me: "Yes, Fanny; I hope I am not later than you expected?"

From her: "Not at all, sir. You always was that punkchel that I used to time myself by you."

It is a detail to state that I had not the remotest idea what she meant by this compliment, especially as I had not made an appointment for any particular hour. However, I did not ask her for an explanation. I addressed her as Fanny quite naturally, and when I followed her into the parlour an odd impression came upon me that I had gone right back into the past, and that I was once more a little boy in pinafores.

The house Mrs. Lemon inhabits is situated in the north of London, in a sadly resigned neighbourhood, which bears a shabby genteel reputation. If I may be allowed such a form of expression I may say that it is respectable in a demi-semi kind of way. I do not mean in respect of its morals, which are unexceptionable, but in respect of its social position. It is situated in a square, and is one of a cluster of tenements so exactly alike in their frontage appearance that were it not for the numbers on the doors a man, that way inclined, might hope for forgiveness for walking in and taking tea with his neighbour's wife instead of with his own. In the centre of the square is an enclosure, bounded by iron railings, which once may have been intended for the cultivation of flowers; at the present time it contains a few ancient shrubs which nobody ever waters, and which are, therefore, always shabby and dusty in dry weather. Even when it rains they do not attempt to put on an air of liveliness; it is as though they had settled down to the conviction that their day is over. To this enclosed rural mockery, each tenant in the square is supposed to have a key, but the only use the ground is put to is to shake carpets in, and every person in or out of the neighbourhood is made free of it, by reason of there being no lock to the gate. There are no signs of absolute poverty in the square. Vagrant children do not play at "shops" on the doorsteps and window-sills; organ men avoid it with a shudder; beggars walk slowly through, and do not linger; peripatetic vendors of food never venture there; and the donkey of the period is unfamiliar with the region. Amusement is provided twice a week by a lanky old gentleman in a long tail coat and a frayed black stock reaching to his ears, whose instrument is a wheezy flute, and whose repertoire consists of "The Last Rose of Summer" and "Away with Melancholy," which he blows out in a fashion so unutterably mournful and dismal as to suggest to the ingenious mind that his nightly wanderings are part of a punishment inflicted upon him at some remote period for the commission of a dark, mysterious crime.

"It's very good of you to come, sir," said Mrs. Lemon, working her right hand slowly backwards and forwards on a faded black silk dress, which I judged had been put on in honour of my visit. "I hope you are well, sir, and your lady, and your precious family."

I replied that my wife and children were quite well, and that we should be glad to see her at any time. When she heard this she burst into tears.

"You always *was* the kindest-hearted gentleman!" 'sobbed. "You never *did* object to being put upon, and you give away your toys that free that all the other children used to take advantage of you. But you didn't mind, sir, not you. Over and over again have your blessed father said when he was alive, 'That boy'll never git along in the world, he's so soft!'" Mrs. Lemon's tears at this reminiscence flowed more freely. "I can't believe, sir, no, I can't believe as time has flown so quick since those happy, happy days!"

The happy days referred to were, of course, the days of my childhood; and my father's prophecy, which I heard now for the first time, respecting my future, brought a contemplative smile to my lips.

"Ah, sir," said Mrs. Lemon, with a sigh, "if we only knew when we was well off, what a lot of troubles we shouldn't have!"

I nodded assent to this little bit of philosophy, and looked round the room, not dreaming that in the humble apartment I was to receive a clue to the mystery of the murder of pretty Lizzie Melladew.

VI

I AM HAUNTED BY THREE EVIL-LOOKING OBJECTS IN MRS. LEMON'S ROOM

It was plentifully furnished: stuffed chairs and couch, the latter with a guilty air about it which seemed to say, "I am not what I seem;" a mahogany table in the centre, upon which was an album which had seen very much better days; ornaments on the mantelshelf, bounded on each corner by a lustre with broken pendants; a faded green carpet on the floor; two pictures on the walls; and on a small table near the window a glass case with an evil-looking bird in it. The pictures were portraits of Mr. and Mrs. Lemon in oil-colour. They appeared to have been recently painted, and I made a remark to that effect.

"Yes, sir," said Mrs. Lemon, in a voice which struck me as being uneasy. "They was done only a few weeks ago." And then, as though the words were forced from her against her will, "Do you see a likeness, sir?"

When she asked this question she was gazing at the portrait of herself.

As a work of art, the painting was a shocking exhibition; as a likeness, it was unmistakable.

"It is," I said, "your very image. Is the portrait of your husband – if that is your husband hanging there —"

She interrupted me with a shudder. "*Hanging* there, sir?"

"I mean on the wall. It *is* a picture of Mr. Lemon, I presume."

"Yes, sir, it's him."

"Is it as faithful a portrait as your own?"

"It's as like him, sir, as two peas. Egscept—" but she suddenly paused.

"Except what, Fanny?"

"Nothing, sir, nothing," she said hurriedly.

If, thought I, it is as like him as two peas, there must be something extraordinarily strange and odd in Mr. Lemon. That he was not a good-looking man could be borne with; but that, of his own free will, he should have submitted to be painted and exhibited with such a sly, sinister expression on his face, was decidedly not in his favour. With his thought in my mind I turned involuntarily to the evil-looking bird in the glass case, and, singularly enough, was struck by an absurd and fearful resemblance between the bird's beak and the man's face. Mrs. Lemon's eyes followed mine.

"Have you had that bird long?" I asked.

"Not long, sir," she replied, and her voice trembled. "About as long as the pictures."

"Did your husband buy it in England? It is a strange bird, and I can't find a name for it."

"Lemon didn't buy it, sir. It was give to him."

I hazarded a guess. "By the artist who painted your husband's portrait?"

"Yes, sir."

Turning from the stuffed bird to the fireplace, I received a shock. In the centre of the mantelshelf was the stone figure of a creature, half monster and half man, with a face bearing such a singular resemblance to Mr. Lemon's and the bird's beak that I rubbed my eyes in bewilderment, believing myself to have suddenly fallen under the influence of a devilish enchantment. But rub my eyes as I might, I could not rub away the strange resemblance. It was no delusion of the senses.

"Was that – that figure, Fanny, given to you by the artist who painted your husband's portrait, and who presented him with that stuffed bird?"

"Yes, sir; he give it to Lemon." And then, in a timorous voice, she asked, "Do you see anything odd in it, sir?"

"It is not only that it's odd," I replied; "but, if you will excuse me for saying so, Fanny, there is really something horrible about it."

In a low tone Mrs. Lemon said, "That's egsactly as I feel, sir."

"Then, why don't you get rid of it?"

"It's more than I dare do, sir. There it is, and there it must remain."

"And there that evil-looking bird is, I suppose, and there that must remain."

"Yes, sir."

"Ah, well," I said, thinking it time to get upon the track, "and now let us talk about something else. You appear to be in trouble."

"You may well say that, sir. I'm worn to skin and bone."

"I'm sorry to hear it, Fanny. Money troubles, I suppose?"

"O, no, sir! We can manage on what we've got, Lemon and me, though he *has* made ducks and drakes with the best part of his savings. Not money troubles, sir; a good deal worser than that."

"Your husband is well, I trust."

"I wish I could say so, sir. No, sir, he's a long way from well, and I didn't know who else to call in, for poor dear Lemon wouldn't stand anybody but you."

Why poor dear Lemon wouldn't stand anybody but me was, to say the least of it, inexplicable; as, since I used to catch indistinct views of his legs when he came courting Fanny in my father's house, I had never set eyes on him. I made no remark, however, but waited quietly for developments.

"He took to his bed, sir," said Mrs. Lemon, "at a quarter to four o'clock yesterday afternoon; and it's my opinion he'll never git up from it."

"That is bad news, Fanny. But your letter to me was written before yesterday afternoon."

"Yes, sir; because I felt that things mustn't be allowed to go on as they *are* going on without trying to alter 'em. They was bad enough when I posted my letter to you, sir; but they're a million times worse now. My blood's a-curdling, sir."

"Eh?" I cried, much startled by this solemn matter-of-fact description of the condition of her blood.

"It's curdling inside me, sir, to think of what is going to happen to Lemon!"

"Come, come, Fanny," I expostulated, "you mustn't take things so seriously; it will not mend them. What does the doctor say?"

"Doctor, sir? Love your heart! If I was to take a doctor into Lemon's room now, I wouldn't answer for the consequences."

"That is all nonsense," I said; "he must be reasoned with."

Mrs. Lemon shook her head triumphantly. "You may reason with some men, sir, and you may delood a child; but reason with Lemon – I defy you, sir!"

There was really no occasion for her to do that, as I was there in the capacity of a friend. While we were conversing I made continual unsuccessful attempts to avoid sight of the objects which had produced upon me so disagreeable an impression, but I could not place myself in such a position as to escape the whole three at one and the same time. If I turned my back upon the evil-looking bird and the portrait of Mr. Lemon, the hideous stone figure on the mantelshelf met my gaze; if I turned my back upon that, I not only had a side view of the bird's beak, but a full-faced view of my friend Lemon. Familiarity with these objects intensified my first impressions of them, and at times I could almost fancy that their sinister features moved in mockery of me. There was in them a fiend-like magnetism I found it impossible to resist.

"Does your husband eat well?" I asked.

"Not so well as he used to do, sir."

"Perhaps," I said, hazarding a guess, "he drinks a little too much."

"No, sir, you're wrong there. He likes a glass – we none of us despise it, sir – but he never exceeds."

"Then, in the name of all that's reasonable, Fanny, what is the matter with him?"

Mrs. Lemon turned to her husband's portrait, turned to the stone figure on the mantelshelf, turned to the evil-looking bird; and her frame was shaken by a strong shuddering.

"Is it anything to do with those objects?" I inquired, my wonder and perplexity growing.

"That's what I want you to find out for me, sir, if I can so fur trespass. Don't refuse me, sir, don't! It's a deal to ask you to do, I know, but I shall be everlastingly grateful."

"I am ready to serve you, Fanny," I said gravely, "but at present I am completely in the dark. For instance, this is the first time I have seen those Mephistophelian-looking objects with which you have chosen to decorate your room."

"I didn't choose, sir. It was done, and I daredn't go agin it."

"I have nothing to say to that; I must wait for your explanation. What I was about to remark was, why that evil-beaked bird—"

"Which I wish," she interposed, "had been burnt before it was stuffed."

"—Should bear so strange a resemblance," I continued, "to the portrait of your husband, and why both should bear so strange a resemblance to the stone monster on your mantel-shelf, is so very much beyond me, that I cannot for the life of me arrive at a satisfactory solution of the mystery. Surely it cannot spring from a diseased imagination, for you have the same fancy as myself."

"It ain't fancy, sir; it's fact. And the sing'lar part of it is that the party as brought them all three into the house is as much like them as they are to each other."

"We're getting on solid ground," I said. "The party who brought them into the house – who gave you the stone monster, who painted your husband's portrait and yours, who stuffed the bird; for, doubtless, he was the taxidermist. An Admirable Crichton, indeed, in the way of accomplishments! You see, Fanny, you are introducing me to new acquaintances. You have not mentioned this party before. A man, I presume."

"I suppose so, sir," she said, with an awestruck look.

"Why suppose?" I asked. "In such a case, supposition is absurd. He is, or is not, a man."

"Let us call him so, sir. It'll make things easier."

"Very much easier, and they will be easier still if you will be more explicit. I seem to be getting more and more in the dark. In looking again upon your portrait, Fanny—"

"Yes, sir?"

"I can almost discern a likeness to—"

"For the merciful Lord's sake, sir," she cried, "don't say that! If I thought so, I should go mad. I'm scared enough already with what has occurred and the trouble I'm in – and Lemon talking in his sleep all the night through, and having the most horrible nightmares – and me trembling and shaking in my bed with what I'm forced to hear – it's unbearable, sir; it's unbearable!"

I was becoming very excited. Unless Mrs. Lemon had lost her senses, there was in this common house a frightful and awful mystery. And Mrs. Lemon had sent for me to fathom it! What was I about to hear – what to discover?

I strove to speak in a calm voice.

"You say your husband took to his bed yesterday, and that you fear he will never rise from it. Then he is in bed at this moment?"

"Yes, sir."

"Where is his bedroom?"

"On the first floor back, sir."

"Can he hear us talking?"

"No, sir."

"And you want me to see him?"

"Before you go, sir, if you have no objections. I sha'n't know how to thank you."

"I will do what I can for you, Fanny. First for your own sake, and next because there appears to be something going on in this house that ought to be brought to light."

"You may well say that, sir. Not only in this house, but out of this house. The good Lord above only knows what *is* going on! But Lemon's done nothing wrong, sir. I won't have him thought badly of, and I won't have him hurt. He's been weak, yes, sir, but he ain't been guilty of a wicked, horrible crime. It ain't in his nature, sir. When I first begun to hear things that he used to say in his sleep, and sometimes when he was awake and lost to everything, my hair used to stand on end. I could feel it stirring up, giving me the creeps all over my skin, and my heart'd beat that quick that it was a mercy it didn't jump out of my body. But after a time, frightened as I was, and getting no satisfaction out of Lemon, who only glared at me when I spoke to him, I thought the time might come – and I ain't sure it won't be this blessed day – when I should have to come forward as a witness to save him from the gallows. I am his wife, sir, and if he ain't fit to look after hisself, it's for me to look after him, and so, sir, I thought the best thing for me to do was to keep a diary."

"A diary!" I echoed, in wonder.

"Yes, sir, a diary – to put down in writing everything what happened at the very time."

"O," I said, "you mean a diary!"

"If that's what you call it, sir. I got an old lodger's book that wasn't all filled up. I keep it locked in my desk, sir. Perhaps you'd like to look at it?"

"It may be as well, Fanny."

"If," she said, fumbling in her pocket for a key, and placing one by one upon the table the most extraordinary collection of oddments that female pocket was ever called upon to hold, "if, when we come into this house to retire and live genteel, after Lemon had sold his business, I'd have known what was to come out of my notion to let the second floor front to a single man, I'd have had my feet cut off before I'd done it. But I did it for the best, to keep down the egspenses. Here it is, sir."

VII

DEVLIN'S FIRST INTRODUCTION INTO THE MYSTERY

She had found the key she had been searching for, and now she opened a mahogany desk, from which she took a penny memorandum-book. She handed it to me in silence, and I turned over the leaves. Most of the pages were filled with weekly accounts of her lodgers, in which "ham and eggs, 8*d.*;" "a rasher, 5*d.*;" "chop, 8*d.*;" "two boyled eggs, 3*d.*;" "bloater, 2*d.*;" "crewet, 4*d.*;" and other such-like items appeared again and again. There was also, at the foot of pages, receipts for payment, "Paid, Fanny Lemon." And this, in the midst of the presumably tragic business upon which we were engaged, brought to my mind an anomaly which had often occurred to me, namely, that landladies should present their accounts to their lodgers in penny memorandum-books, should receive the money, should sign a receipt, and then take away the books containing their acknowledgment of payment. In view of the grave issues impending, it is a trivial matter to comment upon, but it was really a relief to me to dwell for a moment or two upon it. At the end of the memorandum-book which I was looking through were five or six leaves which had not been utilised for lodgers' accounts, and these Mrs. Lemon had pressed into service for her diary. She was a bad writer and an indifferent speller, and the entries were brief, and, to me, at that point, incomprehensible.

"I see, Fanny," I said "that your first entry is made on a Thursday, a good many weeks ago."

"Yes, sir."

"I must confess I can make nothing of it. It states that Lemon rose at eight o'clock on that morning, that he had breakfast at half-past eight, that he ate four slices of bread and butter, two rashers of bacon, and two eggs—"

"Ah!" sighed Mrs. Lemon, interrupting me. "He had his appetite then, had Lemon! He ain't got none now to speak of."

"And," I continued, "that he went out of the house at nine o'clock with a person whose name is unintelligible. It commences, I think, with a D."

"D-e-v-l-i-n," said Mrs. Lemon, her eyes almost starting out of her head as she spelt the name, letter by letter.

"I can make it out now. That is it, Devlin. A peculiar name, Fanny."

"Everything about him is that, sir, and worse."

"Had it been a common name, I daresay I should have made it out at once. Now, Fanny, who is this Devlin?"

"You called him a man, sir," said Mrs. Lemon, striving unsuccessfully to keep her eyes from the portrait of her husband, from the evil-beaked bird, and from the image of the stone monster on the mantelshelf.

The magnetism was not in her, it was in the objects, and as she turned from one to the other I also turned – as though I were a piece of machinery and she was setting me in motion. But it is likely that my eyes would have wandered in those directions without her silent prompting. One peculiarity of the fascination –growing more horrible every moment – exercised by the three objects, was that I could not look upon the one without being compelled to complete the triangle formed by the positions in which they were placed – the wall, the window, the mantel-shelf.

"It was Devlin, then," I said, "who painted the portraits and stuffed the bird and gave you the stone monster?"

"You've guessed it, sir. It was him."

Referring to the entry in the memorandum-book, I asked, "Did this Devlin call for your husband on the Thursday morning that they went out together?"

"No, sir, he lodged here."

"Does he lodge here now?"

"Yes, sir, I am sorry to say. If I could only see the last of him I'd give thanks on my bended knees morning, noon, and night."

"Why don't you get rid of him, then?"

"I can't, sir."

I accepted this as part of the mystery, and did not press her on the point, but I asked why she would feel so grateful if he were gone from the house.

"Because," she replied, "it's all through him that Lemon is as he is."

"Am I to see this man before I leave?"

"It ain't for me to say, sir."

"Is he in the house now?"

"No, sir."

I inwardly resolved if he came into the house before I left it, that I would see the man of whom Mrs. Lemon so evidently stood in dread.

"I suppose, Fanny, you will tell me something more of him."

"That is why I asked you to come, sir. If you're to do any good in this dreadful affair, you must know as much as I do about him."

"Very well, Fanny." I referred again to the first entry in the diary. "After stating that your husband went out with Devlin at nine o'clock in the morning, you say that he returned alone at six o'clock in the evening, and that he did not stir out of the house again on that night."

"Yes, sir."

"I see that you have made a record of the time Lemon went to bed and the time he rose next morning."

"To which, sir, I am ready to take my gospel oath."

"Supposing your gospel oath to be necessary."

"It might be. God only knows!"

I stared at her, beginning to doubt whether she was sane; but there was nothing in her face to justify my suspicion. The expression I saw on it was one of solemn, painful, intense earnestness.

"Go on, sir," she said, "if you please."

I turned again to the concluding words of the first entry, and read them aloud:

"Devlin did not come home all night. I locked the street-door myself, and put up the chain. I went down at seven in the morning, when Lemon was asleep, and the chain was up. I went to Devlin's room, the second floor front, and Devlin was not there!"

"That's true, sir. I can take my gospel oath of that."

"Fanny," I said, with the little book in my hand, closed, but keeping my forefinger between the leaves upon which the first entry was made, "I cannot go any farther until you tell me what all this means."

"After you've finished what I wrote, sir," was her reply, "I'll make a clean breast of it, and tell you everything, or as much of it as I can remember, from the time you saw me last – a good many years ago, wasn't it, sir? – up to this very day."

I thought it best to humour her, and I looked through the remaining entries. They were all of the same kind. Mr. Lemon rose in the morning at such a time; he had breakfast at such a time; he went out at such a time, with or without Devlin; he came home at such a time, with or without Devlin; and so on, and so on. It was a peculiar feature in these entries that Lemon never went out or came home without Devlin's name being mentioned.

I handed the book back to her; she took it irresolutely, and asked,

"Did you read what I last wrote, sir?"

"Yes, Fanny, the usual thing."

"Perhaps, sir, but the time I wrote it; that is what I mean."

"No, Fanny, I don't think I noticed that."

"It was wrote yesterday, sir, and it fixes the time that Lemon came home on Friday, and that he didn't stir out of the house all the night. If I can swear to anything, sir, I can swear to that. Lemon never crossed the street-door from the minute he came in on Friday to the minute he went out agin yesterday. If it was the last word I spoke, I'd swear to it, and it's the truth, and nothing but the truth, so help me God!"

I was about to inquire why she laid such particular stress upon these recent movements of her husband, when there flashed into her eyes an expression of such absolute terror and horror that my first thought was that a spectre had entered the room noiselessly, and was standing at my back. Before I had time to turn and look, Mrs. Lemon clutched my arm, and gasped,

"Do you hear that? Do you hear that?"

VIII

I MAKE THE ACQUAINTANCE OF GEORGE CARTON'S GUARDIAN, MR. KENNETH DOWSETT

I heard something certainly which by this time, unhappily, was neither new nor strange. It was the voice of a newsboy calling out the last edition of a newspaper which, he asserted with stentorian lungs, contained further particulars of the awful murder in Victoria Park. Amid all the jargon he was bawling out, there were really only three words clearly distinguishable. "Murder! Awful murder! Discoveries! Awful discoveries!"

"Are you alarmed, Fanny," I asked, "by what that boy is calling out?"

"Yes," she replied in a whisper, "it is that, it is that!"

"But you must be familiar with the cry," I observed. "There isn't a street in London that was not ringing with it all yesterday."

"It don't matter, it don't matter!" she gasped, in the most inexplicable state of agitation I had ever beheld. "Lemon never stirred out of the house. I'll take my solemn oath of it – my solemn oath."

I released myself from her grasp, and, running into the square, caught up with the newsvendor and bought a paper. Before I returned to the house I satisfied myself that the paper contained nothing new in the shape of intelligence relating to the murder of my friend Melladew's daughter. What the man had bawled out was merely a trick to dispose of his wares. I had reached the doorstep of Fanny's house when my attention was arrested by the figures of two men on the opposite side of the road. One was a man of middle age, and was a stranger to me. In his companion I immediately recognised George Carton. The elder man appeared to be endeavouring to prevail upon George Carton to leave the square, but his arguments had no effect upon Carton, who, shaking him off, hurried across the road to speak to me. His companion followed him.

"Any news, sir?" cried George Carton. "Have you discovered anything?"

"Nothing," I replied, not pausing to inquire why he should put a question so direct to me.

"Nothing!" he muttered. "Nothing! But it shall be brought to light – it shall, or I will not live!"

"Come, come, my dear boy," said the elder man. "What is the use of going on in this frantic manner? It won't better things."

"How am I to be sure of that?" retorted Carton. "It won't better things to stand idly aside, and think and think about it without ever moving a step."

"My ward knows you, sir," said Carton's friend, "and I confess I was endeavouring to persuade him to come home with me when you were running after the newspaper boy. He insisted that your sudden appearance in this square was a strange and eventful coincidence."

"A strange and eventful coincidence!" I exclaimed, and thought, without giving my thought expression, that there was something strange in the circumstance of my being in Fanny Lemon's house, about to listen to a revelation which was not unlikely to have some bearing upon the tragic event, and in being thus unexpectedly confronted by the young man who was to have been married to the murdered girl.

"Yes, that is his idea," said Carton's friend; "but I am really forgetting my manners. Allow me to introduce myself. You are acquainted with my ward, George Carton, the dearest, most generous-hearted, most magnanimous young fellow in the world. I have the happiness to be his guardian. My name is Kenneth Dowsett."

He was a smiling, fair-faced man, with blue, dreamy eyes, and his voice and manners were most agreeable. I murmured that I was very pleased to make his acquaintance.

"My ward," continued Mr. Dowsett, laying his hand affectionately on Carton's shoulder, "has also an odd idea in reference to this dreadful affair, that something significant and pregnant will be discovered in an odd and unaccountable fashion. Heaven knows, I don't want to deprive him of any consolation he can derive from his imaginings. I have too sincere a love for him; but I am a man of the world, and it grieves me to see him indulge in fancies which can lead to no good result. To tell you the honest truth," Mr. Dowsett whispered to me, "I am afraid to let him out of my sight for fear he should do violence to himself."

"My dear guardian," said Carton, "who should know better than I how kind and good you are to me? Who should be better able to appreciate the tenderness and consideration I have always received at your hands? I may be wilful, headstrong, but I am not ungrateful. Indeed, sir" – turning to me – "I am wild with grief and despair, and my guardian has the best of reasons for chiding me. He has only my good at heart, and I am truly sorry to distress him; but I have my ideas – call them fancies if you like – and I must have something to cling to. I will not abandon my pursuit till the murderer is brought to justice, or till I kill him with my own hands!"

"That is how he has been going on," said Mr. Dowsett, "all day yesterday, and the whole live-long night. He hasn't had a moment's sleep."

"Sleep!" cried Carton. "Who could sleep under such agony as I am suffering?"

"But," I said to the young man, whose intense earnestness deepened my sympathy for him, "sleep is necessary. It isn't possible to work without it. There are limits to human strength, and if you wish to be of any service in the clearing up of this mystery, you must conduct yourself with some kind of human wisdom."

"There, my dear lad," said Mr. Dowsett, "doesn't that tally with my advice? I tried to prevail upon him last night to take an opiate—"

"And I wouldn't," interrupted Carton, "and I said I would never forgive you if you administered it to me without my knowledge. Never, never will I take another!" Mr. Dowsett looked at him reproachfully, and the young man added, "There—I beg your pardon. I did not mean to refer to it again."

"If I have erred at all in my behaviour towards you, my dear lad, it is on the side of indulgence. Still," said Mr. Dowsett, addressing me, "that does not mean that I shall give up endeavouring to persuade George to do what is sensible. As matters stand, who is the better judge, he or I? Just look at the state he is in now, and tell me whether he is fit to be trusted alone. My fear is that he will break down entirely."

"I agree with your guardian," I said to Carton; "he is your best adviser."

"I know, I know," said the young man, "and I ought to be ashamed of myself for causing him so much uneasiness. But, after all, sir, I am not altogether in the wrong. I saw Mr. Portland last night, and he said that you and he had had an important interview about this dreadful occurrence."

"I was not aware," I observed, "that you were acquainted with any of the elder members of your poor Lizzie's family."

"I was not," rejoined Carton, "till last night. I introduced myself to Mr. Portland, and told him all that had passed between poor Lizzie and me. I did not have courage enough to go and see Mr. and Mrs. Melladew, but Mr. Portland was very kind to me, and he said that you had undertaken to unravel the mystery."

I did not contradict this unauthorised statement on the part of Mr. Portland, not wishing to get into an argument and prolong the conversation unnecessarily; indeed, it would have been disingenuous to say anything to the contrary, for it really seemed to me in some dim way that I was on the threshold of a discovery in connection with the murder.

"Hearing this welcome news from Mr. Portland," continued Carton, "you would not have me believe that my meeting with you now in a square I never remember to have passed through in my life is accidental? No, there is more in it than you or I can explain."

"What brought you here, then?" I inquired. "Were you aware I was in this neighbourhood?"

"No," replied Carton, "I had not the slightest idea of it."

"He followed the newsboy," explained Mr. Dowsett, "of whom you bought a paper just now. These people, crying out the dreadful news, excercise a kind of fascination over my dear George. I give you my word, he seems to be in a waking dream as he follows in their footsteps."

"I am in no dream," said Carton. "I am on the alert, on the watch. I gaze at the face of every man and woman I pass for signs of guilt. Where is the murderer, the monster who took the life of my poor girl? Not in hiding! It would draw suspicion upon him. He is in the streets, and I may meet him. If I do, if I do—"

"You see," whispered Mr. Dowsett to me, "how easy it would be for him to get into serious trouble if he had not a friend at his elbow."

"What good," I said, addressing Carton, "can you, in reason, expect to accomplish by wearing yourself out in the way you are doing?"

"It will lead me to the end," replied Carton, putting his hand to his forehead; and there was in his tone, despite his denial, a dreaminess which confirmed Mr. Dowsett's remark, "and then I do not care what becomes of me!"

Mr. Dowsett gazed at his ward solicitously, and passed his arm around him sympathisingly.

"Would it be a liberty, sir," said Carton, "to ask what brings you here?"

"I came on a visit to an old friend," I replied evasively, "whom I have not seen for years, and who wished to consult me upon her private affairs."

"Pardon me for my rudeness," he said, with a pitiful, deprecatory movement of his shoulders. "In what you have undertaken for Mr. Portland, will you accept my assistance?"

"If I see that it is likely to be of any service, yes, most certainly."

"Give me something to do," he said in a husky tone, "give me some clue to follow. This suspense is maddening."

"I will do what I can. And now I must leave you. My friend will wonder what is detaining me."

"But one word more, sir. Have you heard any news of Mary?"

"None. So far as I know, she is still missing. If we could find her we should, perhaps, learn the truth."

"Should you need me," said Carton, "you know my address. I gave you my card yesterday, but you may have mislaid it. Here is another. I live with my guardian. It is a good thing for me that I am not left alone. But, good God! what am I saying? I *am* alone – alone! My Lizzie, my poor Lizzie, is dead!"

As I turned into the house I caught a last sight of him standing irresolutely on the pavement, his guardian in the kindest and tenderest manner striving to draw him away.

Fanny was waiting for me at the door of her little parlour. There was a wild apprehensive look in her eyes as they rested on my face.

"What has kep you so long, sir?" she asked in a low tone of fear.

"I came across an acquaintance accidentally," I replied.

"A policeman, sir, or a detective?"

"Good heavens, neither!" I exclaimed.

A sigh of relief escaped her, but immediately afterwards she became anxious again.

"You was talking a long time, sir."

"It was not my fault, Fanny."

"Was – was Lemon's name mentioned, sir?"

"No."

"Was there nothing said about him?"

"Not a word."

This assurance plainly took a weight from her mind. She glanced at the paper I held in my hand, and said:

"Is there anything new in it, sir? Is the murderer caught?"

"No," I replied; "the paper contains nothing that has not appeared in a hundred other newspapers yesterday and today. Fanny, I am about to speak to you now very seriously."

"I'm listening, sir."

"Has Mr. Lemon, your husband, anything to do with this dreadful deed?"

"He had no hand in it, sir, as I hope for mercy! I'll tell you everything I know, as I said I would; but it must be in my own way, and you mustn't interrupt me."

I decided that it would be useless to put any further questions to her, and that I had best listen patiently to what she was about to impart. I told her that I would give her my best attention, and I solemnly impressed upon her the necessity of concealing nothing from me. She nodded, and pouring out a glass of water, drank it off. A silence of two or three minutes intervened before she had sufficiently composed herself to commence, and during that silence the feeling grew strong within me that Providence had directed my steps to her house.

The tale she related I now set down in her own words as nearly as I can recall them. Of all the stories I had ever heard or read, this which she now imparted to me was the most fantastic and weird, and it led directly to a result which to the last hour of my life I shall think of with wonder and amazement.

IX

FANNY LEMON RELATES UNDER WHAT CIRCUMSTANCES SHE RESOLVED TO LET HER SECOND FLOOR FRONT

"I must go back sir," she commenced, "a few years, else you won't be able to understand it properly. I'll run over them years as quick as possible, and won't say more about 'em than is necessary, because I know you are as anxious as I am to come to the horrible thing that has just happened. I was a happy woman in your angel father's house, but when Lemon come a-courting me I got that unsettled that I hardly knew what I was about. Well, sir, as you know, we got married, and I thought I was made for life, and that honey was to be my portion evermore. I soon found out my mistake, though I don't suppose I had more to complain of than other women. In the early days things went fairly well between me and Lemon. We had our little fallouts and our little differences, but they was soon made up. We ain't angels, sir, any of us, and when we're tied together we soon find it out. I daresay it's much of a muchness on the men's side as well as on our'n. Lemon is quick-tempered, but it's all over in a minute, and he forgets and forgives. Leastways, that is how it used to be with him; he would fly out at me like a flash of lightning, and be sorry for it afterwards; and one good thing in him was that he never sulked and never brooded. It ain't so now; he's growed that irritable that it takes more than a woman's patience to bear with him; he won't stand contradiction, and the littlest of things'll frighten him and make him as weak as a child unborn. There was only a couple of nights ago. He'd been going on that strange that it was as much as I could do to keep from screaming out loud and alarming the neighbourhood, and right in the middle of it all he fell asleep quite sudden. It was heavenly not to hear the sound of his voice, but I couldn't help pitying him when I saw him laying there, with the perspiration starting out of his forehead, and I took a cool handkerchief and wiped the damp away, and smoothed his hair back from his eyes.

"He woke up as sudden as he went off, and when he felt my hand on his head he burst out crying and begged me to forgive him. Not for the way he'd been storming at me – no, sir, he didn't beg my forgiveness for that, but for something else he wouldn't or couldn't understandingly explain."

"'What do you mean by it all?' I said. 'What do you mean by it all?'

"But though I as good as went on my bended knees to get it out of him, it wasn't a bit of good. I might as well have spoke to a stone stature. Lemon's had a scare, sir, a frightful awful scare, and I don't know what to think.

"When I married him, sir, he kep a saloon, as I daresay you remember hearing of; shaving threepence, haircutting fourpence, shampooing ditter. He had a wax lady's head in the winder as went round by machinery, and Lemon kep it regularly wound up with her hair dressed that elegant that it would have been a credit to Burlington Arcade. There used to be a crowd round his winder all day long, and girls and boys 'd come a long way to have a good look at it; and though I say it, she was worth looking at. Her lips was like bits of red coral, and you could see her white teeth through 'em; her skin was that pearly and her cheeks that rosy as I never saw equalled; and as for her eyes, sir, they was that blue that they had to be seen to be believed. She carried her head on one side as she went round and round, looking slantways over her right shoulder, and, taking her altogether, she was as prittya exhibition as you could see anywhere in London. It brought customers to Lemon, there was no doubt of that; he was doing a splendid trade, and we put by a matter of between four and five pounds a week after all expenses paid. It *did* go again me, I own, when I discovered that Lemon had female customers, and, what's more, a private room set apart to do 'em up in; but when I spoke to him about he said, with a stern eye:

"'What do you object to? The ladies?'

"'Not so much the ladies, Lemon,' I answered, 'as the private room.'

"'O,' said he, 'the private room?'

"'Yes,' said I; 'I don't think it proper.'

"'Don't you?' said he, getting nasty. 'Well, I do, and there's a end of it. You mind your business, Fanny, and I'll mind mine.'

"I saw that he meant it and didn't intend to give way, and I consequenchually held my tongue. Even when I was told that Lemon often went out to private houses to dress ladies' hair I thought it best to say nothing. I had my feelings, but I kep 'em to myself. I'm for peace and harmony, sir, and I wish everybody was like me.

"One night Lemon give me a most agreeable surprise. He came home and said:

"'Fanny, what would you like best in the world?'

"There was a question to put to a woman! I thought of everything, without giving anything a name. The truth is I was knocked over, so to speak.

"Lemon spoke up agin. 'What would you say, Fanny, if I told you I was going to sell the business and retire?'

"'No, Lemon!' I cried, for I thought, he was trying me with one of his jokes.

"'Yes, Fanny,' he said, 'it's what I've made up my mind to. I've been thinking of it a long time, and now I'm going to do it.'

"I saw that he was in real rightdown earnest, and I was that glad that I can't egspress.

"'Lemon,' I said, when I got cool, 'can we afford it?'

"'Old woman,' he answered 'we've got a matter of a hundred and fifty pound a year to live on, and if that ain't enough for the enjoyment of life, I should like to know how much more you want?'

"He had his light moments had Lemon before certain things happened. People as didn't know him well thought him nothing but a grumpy, crusty man. Well, sir, he *was* that mostly, but with them as was intimate he cracked his joke now and then, and it used to do my heart good to hear him.

"So it was settled, sir. Lemon actually sold his business, and we retired. Five year ago almost to the very day we took this house and become fashionable.

"It was a bit dull at first. Lemon missed his shop, and his customers, and his wax lady, that he'd growed to look upon almost like flesh and blood; but he practised on my head for hours together with his crimping irons and curling tongs, and that consoled him a little. He used to pretend it was all real, and that I was one of his reg'lars, and while he was gitting his things ready he'd speak about the weather and the news in a manner quite perfessional. When he come into the room of a morning at eleven or twelve o'clock with his white apern on and his comb stuck in his hair, and say, 'Good morning, ma'am, a beautiful day,' – which was the way he always begun, whether it was raining or not – I'd take my seat instanter in the chair, and he'd begin to operate. I humoured him, sir! it was my duty to; and though he often screwed my hair that tight round the tongs that I felt as if my eyes was starting out of my head, I never so much as murmured.

"We went on in this way for nearly three years, and then Lemon took another turn. Being retired, and living, like gentlefolk, on our income, we got any number of circulars, and among 'em a lot about companies, and how to make thousands of pounds without risking a penny. I never properly understood how it came about; all I know is that Lemon used to set poring over the papers and writing down figgers and adding 'em up, and that at last he got speculating and dabbling and talking wild about making millions. From that time he spoke about nothing but Turks, and Peruvians, and Egyptians, and Bulls, and Bears, and goodness only knows what other outlandish things; and sometimes he'd come home smiling, and sometimes in such a dreadful temper that I was afraid to say a word to him. One thing, after a little while, I did understand, and that was that Lemon was losing money instead of making it by his goings on with his Turks, and Peruvians, and Egyptians, and his Bulls and Bears; and as I was beginning to git frightened as to how it was all going to end, I plucked up courage to say,

"'Lemon, is it worth while?'

"And all the thanks I got was,

"'Jest you hold your tongue. Haven't I got enough to worrit me that you must come nagging at me?'

"He snapped me up so savage that I didn't dare to say another word, but before a year was out he sung to another tune. He confessed to me with tears in his eyes that he'd been chizzled out of half the money we retired on, and it was a blessed relief to me to hear him say,

"'I've done with it, Fanny, forever. They don't rob me no longer with their Bulls and their Bears.'

"'A joyful hour it is to me. Lemon,' I cried, 'to hear them words. The life I've led since you took up with Bulls and Bears and all the other trash, there's no describing. But now we can be comfortable once more. Never mind the money you've lost; I'll make it up somehow.'

"It was then I got the idea of letting the second floor front. As it's turned out, sir, it was the very worst idea that ever got into my head, and what it's going to lead to the Lord above only knows."

X

DEVLIN THE BARBER TAKES FANNY'S FIRST FLOOR FRONT

"Our first lodger, sir, was a clerk in the City, and he played the bassoon that excruciating that our lives become a torment. The neighbours all complained, and threatened to bring me and Lemon and the young man and his bassoon before the magestrates. I told the clerk that he'd have to give up the second floor front or the bassoon, and that he might take his choice. He took his choice, and went away owing me one pound fourteen, and I haven't seen the colour of his money from that day to this.

"Our second lodger was a printer, who worked all night and slep all day. I could have stood him if it hadn't turned out that he'd run away from his wife, who found out where he was living, and give us no peace. She was a dreadful creature, and I never saw her sober. She smelt of gin that strong that you knew a mile off when she was coming. 'That's why I left her, Mrs. Lemon,' the poor man said to me; 'she's been the ruin of me. Three homes has she sold up, and she's that disgraced me that it makes me wild to hear the sound of her voice. The law won't help me, and what am I to do?' I made him a cup of tea, and said I was very sorry for him, but that she wasn't *my* wife, and that I'd take it kind of him if he'd find some other lodgings. All he said was, 'Very well, Mrs. Lemon, I can't blame you;

but don't be surprised if you read in the papers one day that I am brought up for being the death of her, or that I've made a hole in the water. If she goes on much longer, one of them things is sure to happen.' He went away sorrowful, and paid me honourable to the last farthing.

"It wasn't encouraging, sir, but I didn't lose heart. 'The third time's lucky,' I said to myself, as I put the bill in the winder agin, little dreaming what was to come of it. It remained there nigh on a fortnight, when a knock come at the street-door.

"I do all the work in the house myself. A body may be genteel without keeping a parcel of servants to eat you out of house and home, and sauce you in the bargain. A knock come at the street-door, as I said. If I'd known what I know now, the party as knocked might have knocked till he was blue in the face, or dropped down in a fit before he'd got me to answer him. But I had no suspicions, and I went and opened the door, and there I saw a tall, dark man, with a black moustache, curled up at the ends.

"'You've got a bill in the winder,' said he, 'of a room to let.'

"'Yes, sir,' I answered, hardly giving myself time to look at him, I was that glad of the chance of letting the room; 'would you like to see it?'

"'I should,' said he.

"And in he walked, and up the stairs, after me, to the second floor front. It didn't strike me at the time, but it did often afterwards when I listened for 'em in vain, that I didn't hear his footsteps as he follered me upstairs. Never, from the moment he entered this house, have I heard the least sound from his feet, and yet he wears what looks like boots. He's never asked me to clean 'em, and I'd rather be torn to pieces with red hot pinchers than do it now.

"'It's a cheerful room, sir,' said I to him. 'Looks out on the square.'

"'Charming,' he said, 'the room, the square, you, everything.'

"'That's a funny way of talking,' I thought, and I said out loud, 'Do you think it will suit, sir?'

"'Do I think it will suit?' he said. 'I am sure it will suit. I take it from this minute. What's the rent?'

"'With attendance, sir?' I asked.

"'With or without attendance,' he answered; 'it matters not.'

"Not 'It don't matter,' as ordinary people say, but 'It matters not,' for all the world like one of them foreign fellers we see on the stage. I told him the rent, reckoning attendance, and he said:

"'Good. The bargain is made. I am yours, and you are mine.'

"And then he laughed in a way that almost made my hair stand on end. It wasn't the laugh of a human creature; there was something unearthly about it. As a rule, a body's pleased when another body laughs, but this laugh made me shiver all over; you know the sensation, sir, like cold water running down your back. Then, and a good many times since when he's been speaking or laughing, I felt myself turn faint with sech a swimming sensation that I had to ketch hold of something to keep myself from sinking to the ground.

"'I beg your pardon, sir,' I said, when I come to, 'but if you've no objections I'd like a reference.'

"'Of course you would,' he said, laughing again, 'and here it is.'

"With that he gives me a sovering, and orders me to light the fire. There's that about him as makes it unpossible not to do as he orders you to, so on my knees I went there and then, and lit the fire.

"'Good,' he said. 'I couldn't have done it better myself. Mrs. Lemon – ' and you might have knocked me down with a feather when I heard him speak my name. How did he get to know it? *I* never told him. – Mrs. Lemon,' said he, 'I see in your face that you'd like to ask me a question or two.'

"'I would, sir,' I said, shaking and trembling all over. 'If I may make so bold, sir, are you a married man?'

"He put his hand on his heart, and, grinning all over his face, answered, 'Mrs. Lemon, I am, and have ever been, single.'

"'Might I be so bold as to ask your name, sir?' I said.

"'Devlin,' said he.

"'Dev – what?' I garsped.

"'Lin,' said he. 'Devlin. I'll spell it for you. D-e-v-l-i-n. Have you got it well in your mind?'

"'I have, sir,' I said, very faint.

"'Good,' said he, pointing to the door. 'Go.'

"I had to go, sir, and I went, and that is how Mr. Devlin become our lodger."

XI

DEVLIN PERFORMS SOME WONDERFUL TRICKS, FASCINATES MR. LEMON, AND STRIKES TERROR TO THE SOUL OF FANNY LEMON

"That very night Mr. Devlin come down to this room, without 'with your leave or by your leave,' where Lemon and me was setting, having our regular game of cribbage for a ha'penny a game, and droring a chair up to the table, he begun to talk as though he'd known us all his life. And he can talk, sir, by the hour, and it never seens to tire him, whatever it does with other people. Lemon was took with him, and couldn't keep his eyes off him. No more could I, sir. No more could you if he was here. You might try your hardest, but it wouldn't be a bit of good. There's something in him as forces you to look at him – just as there's something in that bird, and the stone figger on the mantelshelf, and Lemon's portrait as forces you to look at *them*. I've found out the reason of that. When Devlin ain't here *he leaves his sperrit behind him* – that's how it is. I was never frightened of the dark before he come into the house, but now the very thought of going into a room of a night without a candle makes me shiver. And many and many's the time as I've been going upstairs that I've turned that faint there's no describing. He's been behind me, sir, coming up after me, step by step. I can't see him, I can't hear him, but I feel him; and yet there ain't a soul in sight but me. At them times I'm frightened to look at the wall for fear of seeing his shadder.

"Well, sir, on the night that he come into this parlour he goes on talking and talking, and then proposes a hand at cribbage, which Lemon was only too glad to say yes to.

"'Mrs. Lemon must play,' said Devlin; 'we'll have a three-handed game.'

"I shouldn't have minded being left out, especially as our cribbage-board only pegs for two, but his word was lore. So we begun to play, and Devlin marks his score with a red pencil.

"The things he did while we played made my flesh creep. He threw out his card for crib without looking at it, and told us how much was in crib while the cards was laying backs up on the table; and when Lemon and me, both of us slow counters, began to reckon what we had in our hands, Mr. Devlin, like a flash of lightning, cried out how many we was to take. We played five games, and he won 'em all. Then he said he'd show us some tricks. Sir, the like of them tricks was never seen before or since. I've seen conjurers in my time, but not one who could hold a candle to Mr. Devlin. He made the cards fly all over the room, and while he held the pack in his hand and you was looking at 'em, they'd disappear before your very eyes.

"'Where would you like 'em to be?' he asked. 'Underneath you, on your chair? Git up; you're sitting on 'em. In your workbox? Open it and behold 'em.'

"And there they was, sir, sure enough, underneath me, though I'd never stirred from my seat, or in my workbox, which was at the other end of the room. It wasn't conjuring, sir, it was something I can't put a name to, and it wasn't natural. I could hardly move for fright, and as I looked at Mr. Devlin, he seemed to grow taller and thinner, and his black eyes become blacker, and his moustaches curled up to his nose till they as good as met. But Lemon didn't feel as I felt; he was that delighted that he kep on crying –

"'Wonderful! Beautiful! Do it agin, Mr. Devlin, do it agin. Show us another.'

"I don't know when I've seen him so excited; that Devlin had bewitched him.

"'We're brothers you and me,' said Devlin to him. 'I am yours, and you are mine, and we'll never part.'

"The very words, sir, he'd used to me."

"'Hooray!' cried Lemon, 'we're brothers, you and me, and we'll never, never part.'

"'I once kep a barber's shop myself,' said Devlin.

"'What!' cried Lemon, 'are you one of us?'

"'I am,' said Devlin, 'and I've worked for the best in the trade – for Truefitt and Shipwright, and all the rest of 'em. I've been abroad studying the new styles. I'll show you something as 'll make you open your eyes, something splendid.'

"And before I knew where I was, sir, Devlin, in his shirt-sleeves, had whipped a large towel round my neck, and had my hair all down, and was beginning to dress it. Where he got the towel from, and the combs, and the curling-tongs, and the fire, goodness only knows. I didn't see him take them from nowhere, but there they was on the table, and there was Devlin, with his hands in my hair, frizzling it up and corkscrewing it, and twisting and twirling it, and me setting in the chair for all the world as if I'd been turned into stone. But though I didn't have the power to move, I could think about things, and what come into my head was that the man as had taken the second floor front must be some unearthly creature, sprung from I won't mention where.

"'Do you really believe so?' whispered Devlin in my ear.

"'Believe what?' I asked, though my throat was that hot and dry that I wondered how he could make out what I said.

"'That I am an unearthly creature,' he said softly, 'sprung from a place which shouldn't be mentioned to ears perlite?'

"If I was petrified before, sir, you may guess how I felt when I found out that he knew what I was thinking of.

"'You shouldn't be, you shouldn't be,' he whispered agin.

"'Shouldn't be what?' I managed to git out, though the words almost stuck to the roof of my mouth.

"'Sorry you ever took me as a lodger,' he said with a grin. 'Fye, fye! It isn't grateful of you after sech a good reference as I give you. Something 'll happen to you if you don't mind.'

"Well, sir, it was true I'd thought it, but I'll take my solemn oath I never spoke it. It was jest as though that Devlin had my brains spread open before him, and could see every thought as was passing through 'em. I was so overcome that I as good as swooned away, and I believe I should have gone off in a dead faint if he hadn't put something strong to my nose as made me almost sneeze my head off. And while I was sneezing, there was Devlin and Lemon laughing fit to burst theirselves. All the time he was dressing my hair that sort of thing was going on; there wasn't a thought that come into my head that he didn't tell me of the minute it was there, till he got me into that state that I hardly knew whether I was asleep or awake. At last, sir, he finished me up, and stepping back a little, he waved his hand and said to Lemon,

"'There! what do you think of that?' meaning my hair.

"'Wonderful! Beautiful!' cried Lemon, clapping his hands and jumping up and down in his chair, he was that egscited. 'I never saw nothing like it in all my whole born days. It's a new style – quite a new style, and so taking! The ladies 'll go wild over it. Where did you git it from?'

"'From a place,' said Devlin, grinning right in my face, 'as shall be nameless.'

"'But you'll tell me some day, won't you?' cried Lemon. 'Because there might be other styles there as good as that, and we could make our fortunes out of 'em.'

"'I'll take you there one day,' said Devlin, with an unearthly laugh, 'and you shall see for yourself.'

"'Do, do!' screamed Lemon. 'I'd give anything in the world to go there with you!'

"'Good Lord save him!' I thought, looking at Lemon whose eyes was almost starting out of his head. 'He's going mad, he's going mad!'

"'As to making our fortunes,' Devlin went on, 'why not? It shall be so.'

"'It shall, it shall!' cried Lemon.

"'We'll make hundreds, thousands,' said Devlin.

"'We will, we will!' cried Lemon. 'Fanny shall ride in her own kerridge.'

"'Fanny shall,' said Devlin.

"'The Lord forbid,' I thought, 'that I should ever ride in a kerridge bought at sech a price!'

"I thought more free now that Devlin's hands was not in my hair; he didn't seem to be able to read what I was thinking of so long as we was apart.

"'I bind myself to you,' said Devlin to my poor dear Lemon, 'and you bind yourself to me. The bargain's made. Your hand upon it.'

"Lemon gave him his hand, and whether it was fancy or not, it seemed to me that Devlin grew and grew till he almost touched the ceiling; and that, while he was bending over Lemon and looking down on him, like one of them vampires you've read of, sir. Lemon kep growing smaller and smaller till he was no better than a bag of bones.

"'We go out tomorrer morning,' said Devlin, 'you and me together, to look for a shop. Is it agreed?'

"'It is,' answered Lemon, 'it is.'

"'We will set London on fire,' said Devlin.

"'We will, we will,' said Lemon; 'and we'll have shops all over it.'

"'You're a man of sperrit,' said Devlin. 'I kiss your hand.'

"He said that to me; but I clapped my hands behind my back.

"'If you refuse,' said Devlin, smiling at me all the while, 'I must show Lemon another style.'

"And he made as though he was about to dress my hair agin.

"'No, no!' I screamed; 'anything but that, anything but that!"

"I give him my hand, and he kissed it. His mouth was like burning hot coals, and I wondered I wasn't scarred.

"'Don't forgit,' said Lemon, 'tomorrow morning.'

"'I'll not forgit,' said Devlin. 'Till then, adoo.'

"The next minute he was gone.

"No sooner did he close the door behind him than I felt as if tons weight had been lifted off me. I started up, and put my hands to my hair, intending to pull it down.

"'What are you doing?' cried Lemon, starting up too, and seizing hold of me. 'Don't touch it – don't touch it! I must study the style. I never saw sech a thing in all my life. It's more than wonderful, its stoopendous. You look like another woman. Jest take a sight of yerself in the glass.'

"I did take a sight of myself in the glass, and if you'll believe me, sir, it seemed as if my head was covered with millions of little serpents, curling and twisting all sorts of ways at once; and, as I looked at 'em moving, sir – which might have been or might not have been, but so it was to me – I saw millions of eyes shining and glaring at me.

"'O, Lemon, Lemon!' I cried, bursting out into tears; 'what *have* you done, what *have* you done?'

"'Done?' said Lemon, rubbing his hands; he'd let mine go. 'Why, gone into partnership with the finest hairdresser as ever was seen. Our fortune's made, Fanny, our fortune's made!'

"I tried to reason with him, but I might as well have spoke to stone. He was that worked up that he wouldn't listen to a word I said. All the satisfaction I could git out of him was –

"'A good night's work, Fanny; a good night's work!'

"If he said it once he said it fifty times. But I knew it was the worst night's work Lemon had ever done, and that it'd come to bad. And it has, sir."

XII

FANNY LEMON RELATES HOW HER HUSBAND, AFTER BECOMING BETTER ACQUAINTED WITH DEVLIN THE BARBER, SEEMED TO BE HAUNTED BY SHADOWS AND SPIRITS

"I had my way about my hair before I went to bed. I waited till Lemon was asleep, and then I brushed all the serpents out, and did it up in a plain knot behind. I felt then like a Christian, and I said my prayers before I stepped in between the sheets. I didn't sleep much; Lemon was that restless he torsed and torsed the whole night long, and his eyes was quite bloodshot when he got up. While he was dressing I heard Devlin call out:

"'Lemon, I'm coming down to have breakfast with you.'

"'Do,' cried Lemon. 'You're heartily welcome.'

"I was downstairs at the time – I always git up before Lemon, to make the place straight and cook the breakfast – and I heard what passed. Lemon, half-dressed, come running down to me, and told me to be sure to git something nice for breakfast, and not to cut the rashers too thin.

"'Go to the fish-shop,' he said, 'and git a haddick. We must treat him well, Fanny, or he might cry off the bargain he made with me last night.'

"I thought to myself I knew how I'd treat him if I had my way, but it wouldn't have done jest then for me to go agin Lemon. There was times when he said a thing that it had to be done, and that was one of 'em. So I goes to the fishmonger's and gits a haddick, and I cooks three large rashers and six eggs—three fried and three biled – and then Lemon and Devlin they come in together as thick as thieves. Devlin had been telling Lemon something as had made him laugh till his face was purple.

"'You never heard sech a man,' said Lemon to me. 'He's one in a thousand.'

"'He's one in millions,' I thought, and I kep my head down for fear Devlin should suspect what I was thinking of; 'and there's only one as ever *I* heard of.'

"Devlin give me good morning and shook hands with me; I didn't dare to refuse him. If he'd offered to kiss me, Lemon wouldn't have objected, I believe, though there was a time when he was that jealous of me that a man hardly dared to look at me. But those happy days was gone for ever.

"I didn't have much appetite for breakfast, and no more had Lemon, but Devlin made up for the pair of us. There was the haddick, and there was the three rashers, and there was the six eggs. Devlin pretty well cleared the lot. It was Lemon, I *must* say, who pushed him on to it, though it didn't seem to me as he wanted much persuading. He had the appetite of a shark. It didn't give me no pleasure to hear him praise my cooking and to hear him say to Lemon that he'd got a treasure of a wife.

"'I have,' said Lemon; 'Fanny's a good sort.'

"When breakfast was over and everything cleared away Lemon asked Devlin if he was ready, and Devlin said he was, and they went out arm in arm jest as if they was brothers.

"They come home late, and Lemon was more excited than ever.

"'It's all settled, Fanny,' he said, 'I've taken another shop, and Devlin and me's gone into partnership. We're going to work together, and we'll astonish your weak nerves.'

"As if they hadn't been astonished enough already.

"I asked Lemon where the shop was that he'd taken, but he wouldn't tell me.

"'It's a secret,' he said, 'between Devlin and me. What an egstrordinary man he is, Fanny! What a glorious, glorious fellow! What a fortunate thing that he saw the bill in our winder of a room to let, and that he didn't go somewheres else! It's a providence, Fanny, that's what it is.'

"I wasn't to be put down so easy, and I tried my hardest to git out of Lemon where the shop was, but he wouldn't let on.

"'I've promised Devlin,' he said, 'not to say a word about it to a living soul. Perhaps we sha'n't keep it open long; perhaps we shall shut it up after a month or two and take another; perhaps we shall do a lot of trade at private houses. It's all as Devlin likes. I've give him the lead. There never was sech a man.'

"That was all I could git out of him. Devlin had him tight; 'twas nothing but Devlin this, and Devlin that, and Devlin t'other. Devlin was as close as he was; I couldn't git nothing out of him.

"'I love wimmin,' he said, 'but they must be kep in their place. Eh, Lemon?'

"That was a nice thing for a wife to hear, wasn't it?

"'Yes,' said Lemon: 'you mind your business, Fanny, and we'll mind our'n.'

"They went out the next morning together, and kep out late agin; and so it went on for a matter of four or five weeks. Then therecome a change. From being in love with Devlin, Lemon begun to be frightened of him. I saw it in his face every morning when they went away. Instead of Lemon's taking Devlin's arm as he did at first, it was Devlin who used to take Lemon's arm, jest above the elberjint, as much as to say:

"'I've got you, and I'm not going to let you escape me.'

"And instead of Lemon being brisk and lively and egscited of a morning, as though he was going for an excursion in a pleasure van, he got grumpy and dull, as though he was going to the lock-up to answer for some dreadful thing he'd done. I spoke to him about it, but if he was close before, he was a thousand times closer now.

"'Don't ask me nothing, Fanny,' he'd say; 'don't put questions to me about *him*. I daren't say a word, I daren't, I daren't!'

"That didn't stop me; he was my husband, and if strange things was being done, who had a better right than me to know all about 'em? But it was all no use; I couldn't git nothing out of him.

"'If you don't shut up,' he said, quite savage like, 'I'll set Devlin on to you, and you'll have cause to remember it to the last day of your life!'

"Jest as if I haven't got cause to remember it! If I lived a thousand years I couldn't forgit what's happened.

"If I could have got rid of my lodger I shouldn't have thought twice about it; out he'd have gone; but he paid me reg'lar, did Devlin, and always in advance, so that I had no egscuse for giving him notice. And even if I had, I ain't at all sure that I should have had the courage to do it.

"It begun to trouble me more than I can say, that I never heard him come in or go out, and that I never caught the sound of his footsteps on the stairs or in the passage, and that, when he might have been in the Canary Islands for all I knew, I'd turn my head and see him standing at the back of me, without my having the least idea how he got into the room.

"'Here I am, you see, Mrs. Lemon,' he'd say; 'back agin, like a bad penny. You're glad to see me, I'm sure. Say you're glad.'

"And I had to, whether I liked it or not. Then he'd grin and wag his head at me, and sometimes say if he knew where there was another woman like me he'd stick up to her. 'Lord have mercy,' I used to think, 'on the woman who'd give you a second look unless she was obliged to!'

"I grew to be that shaky and trembly that my life was a perfect misery; and so was Lemon's. But I used to speak about it, which was a little relief, while poor Lemon would never so much as open his lips. I pitied him a deal more than I did myself. I did say to him once:

"'Lemon, let's call a broker in when Devlin's not here, and sell the furniture, and run away.'

"'You talk like a fool,' said Lemon. 'If we was to hide ourselves in the bowels of the earth he'd ferret us out.'

"Then Lemon said one night that Devlin was going to paint our portraits.

"'He sha'n't paint mine,' I cried, 'not if he orfered to frame it in dymens!'

"The words was no sooner out of my lips than I turned almost to a jelly at hearing Devlin's voice at the back of me, saying,

"'Nonsense, nonsense, Mrs. Lemon! Surely it ain't me you're speaking of? Don't they paint all the Court beauties, and ain't you as good as the best of them? Your face is like milk and roses, and I'm the artist that's going to do justice to it. You can't refuse me; you won't have the heart to refuse me.'

"Which I hadn't, with him so close to me. He seemed to take the backbone out of me; I used to feel quite limp when he took me up like that. He *did* paint my picture, and there it is, stuck on the wall; and though it's come over me a hunderd times to drag it down and burn it, it's more than I dare do for fear of something dreadful happening.

"I can't describe what I went through while that picture was being painted. There was I, setting like a stature in the position that Devlin placed me; and there was Lemon, leaning for'ard, with his hands clarsping the arms of his chair, and his eyes glaring like a ghost's; and there was Devlin, waving his brush and painting me, making all sorts of strange remarks, and singing all sorts of songs in all sorts of languages. He could do that, sir; I don't believe there's a language in the world that he can't speak, and I don't believe there's anything in the world, or out of it, for that matter, that he doesn't know. "*Now, where did he get it all from?*

"I used to wonder about his age. It was a regular puzzler. Sometimes he looked quite young, and sometimes he looked as old as Methusalem. I plucked up courage once to ask him.

"'What do you say to twenty?' he answered. 'Or if that won't do, what do you say to eighty, or a couple of hunderd?'

"When my portrait was finished he pretended to go into egstacies over it, and said that it really ought to be egshibited.

"'Mind you keep it as aairloom,' he said. 'You've no notion what it's worth.'

"Then he took Lemon's picture, and it was a comfort to me that he painted my husband upstairs. Every night for a fortnight Lemon went up to Devlin's room, and set there for two or three hours, and then he'd slide into this room looking as if he'd jest come out of his corfin. It give me such a shock when I first saw the picture that I threw my apern over my head.

"'Ah,' said Devlin with a grin, pulling my apern away, 'I thought you'd be overcome when you set eyes on it. It's a rare piece of work, ain't it? Why, it almost speaks!'

"It was as like Lemon as like could be – I couldn't deny that; but there was the sly, wicked look which you've noticed in that there stuffed bird and in the stone image on the mantelshelf. Devlin made us a present of them things after he'd painted the portraits, and told me to treasure 'em for his sake, and that whenever I looked at 'em I was to think of him. He said they was worth ever so much money, but that I was never, never to part with 'em.

"'If you do,' he said, laughing in my face, 'I'll haunt you day and night.'

"So things went on, gitting worser and worser every day, and Lemon got that thin that you could almost blow him away. And now, sir, I'm coming to the most dreadful part of the whole affair, something that has frightened me more than all the rest put together. What I'm going to speak of now is that awful murder in Victoria Park. Don't think I'm making it up out of my head. I ain't clever enough or wicked enough. If I was I should deserve a judgment to fall on me.

"I've told you of Lemon speaking in his sleep – never did he go to bed without saying things in the night that'd send my heart into my mouth. He seemed as if he was haunted by shadders and spirits, and as if there was always something weighing on his soul that he daren't let out when he was awake. When I found it was no good arguing with him I give it up, and I bore with his writhes and groans, without telling him in the morning of the dreadful night I'd passed. But the day before yesterday, sir, things come to a head.

"He went out early with Devlin as usual, and they both come home together a deal later than they was in the habit of doing. I fixed the time in my diary, sir; it was half-past eight o'clock. Before that I'd wrote my letter to you and posted it – the letter you got yesterday morning. Little did I dream of what was going to happen after I sent it off.

"I noticed that Lemon was more trembly than ever, and there was that in his eyes which made my heart bleed for him. It wasn't a wandering look, because he was afraid to look behind him; it was as if he was trying to shut out something horrible. But I didn't say a word to him while Devlin was with us. He didn't remain long.

"'I'm going to my room,' he said; 'I've got a lot of writing to do. Bring me up a pot of tea before you go to bed. Lemon and me's been spending a pleasant hour at the Twisted Cow.'

"'Lemon looks as if he'd been spending a pleasant hour,' I thought, as I looked at his white face.

"Then Devlin went to his room on the second floor, and I breathed more free.

"The Twisted Cow, sir, is a public which Devlin is fond of. You may be sure he'd pick out a house with a outlandish name.

"'O, Lemon, Lemon,' I said, 'you look like a ghost!'

"'Hush!' he said, with his hand to his ear; he was afraid Devlin might be listening. 'Don't speak to me, Fanny; I want to be quiet, very quiet. How horrible, how horrible!'

"'What's horrible. Lemon?' I asked, putting my arms round his neck.

"He pushed me away and asked what I meant.

"'You said "How horrible, how horrible!" jest now, Lemon.'

"To my surprise, he answered 'I didn't. You must have fancied it. Let me be quiet.'

"I didn't dispute with him, and we set here in the parlour for more than an hour without saying a word to each other. Lemon hadn't been drinking, sir; he was as sober as I am this minute.

"'I think I'll go to bed, Fanny,' he said.

"The tears come into my eyes, he spoke so soft.

"'Shall I go and git your supper-beer, Lemon?' I asked.

"'No,' he said, ketching hold of me. 'I won't be left alone in the house with that –that devil upstairs! I don't want no supper-beer.'

"It was the first time he'd ever spoke of Devlin in that way, and I knew that something out of the common must have happened. Perhaps they'd quarrelled. O, how I hoped they had! It might put a end to their partnership, and there would be a chance of peace and happiness once more.

"'I won't leave you. Lemon,' I said. 'I'll take that wretch his tea, and I hope it'll choke him, and then I'll come to bed too. Shall I make you some gruel, Lemon, or anything else you fancy?'

"'No,' he answered. 'I don't want nothing – only to sleep, to sleep!'

"I made the tea for Devlin, and it's a mercy I didn't have any poison in the house, because I might have been tempted to put it in the pot – though perhaps that wouldn't have hurt him. I knocked at his door, and he said as pleasant as pleasant can be, 'Come in, Mrs. Lemon. What a treasure you are! How happy Lemon ought to be with sech a wife!'

"But I didn't stop to talk to him. I put the tea on the table and went down to Lemon. He was already in bed, and his head was covered with the bedclothes.

"'I'll jest run down,' I whispered, 'and put up the chain on the street-door. I won't be a minute. Lemon.'

"I was back in less than that, and I went to bed. Lemon never moved. I spoke to him, but he didn't answer me; and after a little while I went to sleep.

"I woke up as the clock struck twelve all in a prespiration. Lemon was talking in his sleep, and this is what he said:

"'Victoria Park. Eighteen years old. Golden hair. With a bunch of daisies in her belt. A bunch of white daisies, with blood on 'em! With blood on 'em! With blood on 'em! O Lord, have mercy on her! Near the water. Lord, have mercy on her! Lord, have mercy on her!'

"And then, sir, he give a scream that curdled right through me, and cried, 'Don't let him – don't let him! Save her – save her!'

"How would *you* feel, sir, if you heard someone laying by your side saying sech things in the dead of night?"

XIII

IN WHICH FANNY NARRATES HOW HER HUSBAND HAD A FIT, AND WHAT THE DOCTOR THOUGHT OF IT

"Nothing more took place before we got up in the morning. Lemon torsed about as usual, and kept groaning and talking to hisself, but, excep what I've told you, I couldn't make head or tail of his mumblings. Devlin come down to breakfast, and said, as gay as gay can be,

"'I've had a lovely night.'

"'Have you?' said I. I wouldn't have spoke if I could have helped it, but he's got a way of forcing the words out of you.

"'Yes,' he answered, 'a most lovely night. I've slep the sleep of the just.' What he meant by it I don't know, but it's what he said. 'You look tired, Mrs. Lemon.'

"He grinned in my face, sir, as he made the remark, and my blood begun to boil.

"I've got enough to make me look tired,' I said. 'Lemon hasn't had a decent night's rest for months.'

"'You don't say so! But why not, why not?' asked Devlin, pitching into the ham and eggs.

"'You can answer that better than I can,' I said, jumping from the table; 'You; yes, you!'

" 'Fanny!' cried Lemon.

" 'I don't care,' I said, feeling reckless; I think it must have been because I was sure you'd come to my help, sir. 'I don't care. Things aren't as they should be, and it stands to reason they can't go on like this much longer.'

" 'O,' said Devlin, helping hisself to the last rasher. 'It stands to reason, does it?'

" 'Yes, it does,' I answered. 'I'm Lemon's wife, and if he can't take care of hisself it's my duty to do it for him.'

" 'Can't you take care of yourself?' asked Devlin of my poor husband. 'That's sad, very sad!'

" 'I can, I can,' cried Lemon. 'Fanny don't know what she's talking about.'

" 'I thought as much,' said Devlin. 'Nerves unstrung. She wants bracing up. I must prescribe for her.'

" 'Not if I know it,' I said. 'I've had enough of you and your prescribing to last me a lifetime. Don't look at me like that, or you'll drive me mad!'

" 'Was there ever sech an unreasonable woman?' said Devlin, and he come and laid his hand upon me. 'Jest see how she's shaking. Lemon. She's low, very low; I really must prescribe for her. Leave her to me. I'll see that no harm comes to her.'

"What with his great staring eyes piercing me through and through, and his hand patting my shoulder, and his mocking voice, and the grin on his face, all my courage melted clean away, and I burst out crying and run into the kitchen. There I stayed till I heard the street-door slam, and then I went back to clear the breakfast-things, with a thankful heart that Devlin was gone. If he'd only have left my husband behind him I should have been satisfied, but Lemon was gone too. There was a bottle on the table with something in it, and a label on it in Devlin's writing –

"For my dear kind friend, Mrs. Lemon. A tonic for her nerves. A tablespoonful, in water, three times a day.'

"'A tablespoonful, in water, three times a day,' thinks I to myself. 'Not if I know it.'

"I was going to throw the bottle in the dusthole, but I thought I'd better not, and I put it away on the top shelf of the cupboard, right at the back. After that I went about my work, wondering how it was all going to end, and casting about in my mind whether there was anything I could do to get rid of the creature as was making our lives a misery. But I couldn't think of nothing.

"Lemon was never very fond of politics, but he likes to know what's going on, and we take in a penny weekly newspaper as gives all the news from one end of the week to the other, and how they do it for the money beats me holler. The boy brings it every Sunday morning, and it ain't once in a year that Lemon buys a daily paper. You'll see presently why I mention it.

"It was five o'clock in the afternoon, and I was setting sewing when I hears the latchkey in the street-door. Now, Saturday is always a late day with Lemon and Devlin; they don't generally come home till ten or eleven o'clock at night, and I was surprised when I heard the key in the lock. I knew it must be one or the other of 'em, because nobody but them and me has a latchkey. I set and listened, wondering whether it was Lemon and what had brought him home so early, and I made up my mind, if it *was* him, to have a good talk with him, and try and persuade him once more to give up Devlin altogether. 'But why don't he come in?' thought I. There he was in the street, fumbling about with the key as though there was something wrong with it; and he stayed there so long that I couldn't stand it no longer, so I goes to the door and opens it myself. The minute it was open Lemon reels past me, behaving hisself as if he was mad or drunk. I picked up the latchkey which he'd dropped, and follered him into the parlour here. What made him ketch hold of me, and moan, and cry, and look round as if he'd brought a ghost in with him, and it was standing at his elber? And what made him suddingly cover his face with his hands, and after trembling like a aspen leaf, tumble down on the floor in a fit right before my very eyes? There he laid, sir, twisting and foaming, a sight I pray I may never see agin.

"I knelt down quick and undid his neck-handkercher, and tried to bring him to, but he got worse and worse, and all I could do wasn't a bit of good.

"There was nobody in the house but Lemon and me, and, almost distracted, I run like mad to the chemist's shop at the corner of the second turning to the right, who's got a son walking the hospitals, and begged him to come with me and see my poor man. He come at once, sir, and there was Lemon still on the floor in his fit. The doctor unclarsped Lemon's hands and put something in 'em, and I slipped a cold key down his back because his nose was bleeding.

"'That's a good sign,' said the doctor, as he forced Lemon's jaws apart and put a spoon between his teeth, which Lemon almost bit in two. Then he threw a jug of cold water into Lemon's face, completely satcherating him, and after that Lemon wasn't so violent; but he didn't recover his senses or open his eyes.

"'Let's git him to bed,' said the doctor.

"He helped me carry Lemon upstairs, where we undressed him, and it wasn't before we got him between the sheets that he come to.

"'Feel better?' asked the doctor.

"But Lemon never spoke.

"'Don't leave him,' said the doctor to me, and he went back to his shop and brought a sleeping draught, which Lemon took, and soon afterwards fell asleep.

"'He won't wake,' said the doctor, 'for twelve hours at least. Is he subject to fits?'

"'No, sir,' I answered; 'this is the first he's ever had. Can you tell me what's the matter with him? He ain't been drinking, has he?'

"'There's no sign of drink,' said the doctor, 'and no smell of it. *Does* he drink?'

"'Not more than is good for him,' I said. 'I've never seen Lemon the worse for liquor.'

"'What I don't like about him,' the doctor then said, 'was the look in his eyes when he come to his senses – as if he'd had a shock. Has he taken a religious turn?'

"'No, sir.'

"'Is he sooperstitious at all?'

"'No, sir.'

"'The reason I ask, Mrs. Lemon,' said the doctor, 'is because this don't seem to me a ordinary fit. Is there any madness in your husband's family?'

"'I never heard of any,' I answered, 'and I think I should have been sure to know it if there was.'

"'Very likely,' said the doctor, 'though sometimes they keep it dark. All I can say is, there's something on Mr. Lemon's mind, or he's received a mental shock.'

"With that he went away.

"Lemon by that time was sound as a top. The doctor must have given him a strong dose to overcome him so, and it did my heart good to see him laying so peaceful. But I couldn't help thinking over what the doctor had said of him. There was either something on Lemon's mind or he'd received a mental shock. And that was said without the doctor knowing what I knew, for I'd kep my troubles to myself. I didn't as much as whisper what Lemon had said in his sleep the night before about the young girl in Victoria Park with golden hair and a bunch of white daisies in her belt, covered with blood.

"'Perhaps Lemon's been reading a story,' I thought, 'with something like that in it, and it's took hold of him.'

"There was nothing to wonder at in that. The penny newspaper we take in always has a story in it that goes on from week to week, and always ending at such a aggravating part that

I can hardly wait to git the next number. I fly for it the first thing Sunday morning, before I read anything else. Lemon goes for the police-courts, and takes the story afterwards.

"My mind was running on in that way as I picked up Lemon's clothes, which the doctor and me had tore off him and throwed on the floor; and I don't mind telling you, sir, that I felt in the pockets. First, his trousers. There was nothing in 'em but a few coppers and two-and-six in silver. Then his westcoat. There was nothing in that but his silver watch and a button that had come off. Then his coat. What I found there was his handkercher, his spectacles, and a evening newspaper, I folded his clothes tidy, and come downstairs with the paper in my hand. There must be something particular in it, thinks I, as I set down in the parlour here, and opened it in the middle, and smoothed it out. There was, sir.

"The very first words I saw, in big letters, at the top of the column was –'Dreadful and Mysterious Discovery in Victoria Park. Ruthless Murder of a Young Girl. Stabbed to the Heart! A Bunch of Blood-stained Daisies!'

"Can you imagine my feelings, sir?

"I could scarce believe my eyes. But there it was, staring me in the face, like a great bill on the walls printed in red. The ink was black, of course, but as I looked at the awful words they grew larger and larger, and their colour seemed to change to the colour of blood."

XIV

DEVLIN APPEARS SUDDENLY, AND HOLDS A CONVERSATION WITH FANNY ABOUT THE MURDER

"Now, sir, while I was looking in a state of daze at the paper, and trying to pluck up courage to read it, I felt a chill down the small of my back, and I knew that our lodger Devlin had crep into the room unbeknown, without me hearing of him.

"'What is this I've been told as I come along?' he said. 'My friend Lemon, your worthy husband, taken ill? It is sad news. Is he very ill? Let me see him.'

"What did I do, sir, but run out of the room, and upstairs where Lemon was sleeping, and whip out the key from the inside of the door and put it in the outside, and turn the lock. Then I felt I could breathe, and I went downstairs to Devlin.

"'Why do you lock the poor man in?' he asked.

"'How do you know?' I said, 'that I have locked him in, unless you've been spying me?'

"'How do I know what I know?' he said, laughing. 'Ah, if I egsplained you might not understand. Perhaps there's little I don't know. I've travelled the world over, Mrs. Lemon, and there's no saying what I've learnt. As for spying, fye, fye, my dear landlady! But you must be satisfied, I suppose, being a woman. Have you ever heard of second sight? It's a wonderful gift. Perhaps I've got it; perhaps I can see with my eyes shut. Sech things are. But this is trifling. Poor Lemon! I am really concerned for him. You musn't keep me away from him. I'm a doctor, and can do him a power of good.'

"'Not,' I said, and where I got the courage from in the state I was in, goodness only knows, 'while there's breath in my body shall you doctor my husband. Mischief enough you've done; you don't do no more.'

"'Mischief, you foolish woman!' he said. 'What mischief? Have you took leave of your senses?' But I didn't answer him. 'Ah, well,' he said, shrugging his shoulders, 'let it be as you wish with my poor friend Lemon. I yield always to a lady. What is this?' And he took up the newspaper. 'You've been reading, I see, the particulars of this sad case. It is more than sad; it is frightful.'

"'I haven't read it,' I said.

"'But you was going to?'

"'I won't bemean myself by denying it,' I said. 'Yes, I was going to, when you come into the room unbeknown and unbeware.'

"I had it in my mind to say that it was a liberty to come into a room as didn't belong to him without first knocking at the door, but his black eyes was fixed on me and his moustache was curling up to his nose, and I didn't dare to.

"'When I come into the room,' he said, 'unbeknown and unbeware, as you egspress it, you had no ears for anything. You was staring at the paper, and your eyes was wild. What for? Is it a murder that frightens you? Foolish, stupid, because murders are so common. How many people go to bed at night and never rise from it agin, because of what happens while they sleep! This murder is strange in a sort of way, but not clever – no, not clever. A young girl, eighteen years of age, beautiful, very beautiful, with hair of gold and eyes of blue, receives a letter.

From her lover? Who shall say? That is yet to be discovered in the future. "Meet me," the letter says, "in Victoria Park, at the old spot" – which proves, my dear landlady, that they have met before in the same place – "at eleven o'clock tonight." An imprudent hour for a girl so young; but, then, what will not love dare? When you and Lemon was a-courting didn't you meet him whenever he asked you at all sorts of out-of-the-way places? It is what lovers do, without asking why. "And wear," the letter goes on, "in your belt a bunch of white daisies, so that I may know it is you." Now, why that? It is the request of a bungler. If the letter was wrote by her lover – and there is at present no reason to suppose otherwise – he would recognise his sweetheart without a bunch of white daisies in her belt. What, then, is the egsplanation? That, also, is in the future to be discovered. Let us imagine something. Say that between the young girl with the hair of gold and the eyes of blue and the man that writes the letter there is a secret, the discovery of which will be bad for him. Pardon, you wish to ask something?'

"'Yes,' I said, 'about the letter. How do you know it was wrote?'

"'Did I say I know?' he answered, with his slyest, wickedest look. 'Ain't we imagining, simply imagining? Being in the dark, we must find some point to commence at, and nothing can be more natural than a letter.'

"'Was it found in the young lady's pocket?' I asked.

"'Nothing was found,' he answered, 'in the young lady's pocket.'

"'Then it ain't possible,' I said, 'that the letter could have been wrote.'

"'Sweet innocence!' said Devlin, and with all these dreadful goings on, sir, that was making me tremble in my shoes, he had the impidence to chuck me under the chin – and Lemon upstairs in the state he was! 'What could be easier than to empty a young lady's pockets when she's laying dead before you. A job any fool could do. But the letter may be found.'

"'And the murderer, too,' I said, with a shudder, 'and hanged, I hope!'

"'I share your hope,' he said, with one of his strange laughs,' by the neck till he is dead. The more the merrier. To continue our imaginings. Between the young lady and her lover, as I said, there's a secret as would be bad for him if it was made public – as might, indeed, be the ruin of him. This secret may be revealed in the correspondence as passed between them. The chances are that those letters are not destroyed. Men are so indiscreet! Why, they often forgit there's a tomorrer. The young lady is described as being beautiful. More's the pity. Beauty's a snare. If ever I marry – which ain't likely, Mrs. Lemon – I'll marry a fright. Beautiful as the young lady is, her lover wishes to git rid of her. Perhaps he's tired of her; perhaps he's got another fancy; perhaps he's seen her twin sister, and is smit with her. There's any number of perhapses to fit the case. But the poor girl, having been brought to shame—'

"'Is that in the paper?' I asked, interrupting him.

"'No,' he answered, 'but it may be. It is always so with those girls; there's hardly a pin to choose between 'em. Naturally, she won't consent to let him get rid of her – won't consent to release him – won't consent to let him go free. They quarrel, and make it up. They quarrel agin, and make it up agin. Days, weeks go by, till yesterday comes, and she is to meet him at night. She's got a mother, she's got a father; they set together, and she goes to bed early. She's got a headache, she says, and so, "Goodnight, mother; goodnight, father;" a kiss for each of 'em; and there's a end of kisses and goodnights. The last page of her little book of life is reached. There's a lot in that scene to make a body think – it's full of pictures of the past. Think of all the days of childhood wasted; think of all the love, laughter, hopes, joys – wasted; flowers, ribbons, fancies, dreams – wasted; all that good men say is sweetest in life, and that's played its part for so many, many years – all wasted. Better to have been wicked at once, better to have been sinful and deceitful all through – think you not so? "Goodnight, mother; goodnight, father," and so – to bed? No. To go up to her little room and lock the door, to dress herself in her best clothes, to make herself still more beautiful – for that, you see, may melt her lover's heart – to put the bunch of white daisies in her belt, to wait till the house is quiet – so quiet, so quiet! – and then to steal out softly, softly! She stops at mother's door and listens. Not a sound. Mother and father sleep in peace. Remembrances of the past come to her in the dark, and she cries a little, very quietly. Then she departs. It is done. From that home she is gone for ever, and she is walking to her grave! The park is still and quiet at that hour of the night; excep for a few hungry wretches who prowl or sleep, the girl and the man have it all to themselves. First – love passages. Twelve o'clock. They stop and listen to the tolling of the bell – they all do that. Some smile and sing at the chimes, some shiver and groan. Next – arguments, entreaties to be released. He will be so good to her, O, so good, if she will only release him! One o'clock. Next – more love-making and coaxing, then threats, passionate reproaches, defiance. Ah, it has come to that – the end is near! Two o'clock. He stabs her, quick and sudden, to the heart? Hark! do you hear the wild scream? Her body is dead, and her soul – ? But that and other mysteries remain to be unravelled – which may be – Never!'"

XV

FANNY DESCRIBES HOW SHE MADE UP HER MIND WHAT TO DO WITH LEMON

"Devlin put down the newspaper, and waited for me to speak. I think, sir, I've told you egsactly what he said, and as fur as possible in his own words. They are so printed on my mind that I couldn't forgit 'em if I tried ever so hard. As he described what had took place it was as if he was painting pictures, and he made me see 'em. I saw the poor girl's home; I saw her setting with her father and mother in jest sech a little room as this – for they are only humble people, sir; I saw her kiss 'em goodnight; I saw her in her bedroom a-doing herself up before the looking-glass; I saw her put the bunch of white daisies in her belt; I saw her steal out of the house to the park; I saw the man and her walking about among the trees, and sometimes setting down to talk; I heard a scream – another! – another! – and I covered my eyes with my hands to shut it all out. I was so overcome that I hadn't strength to wrench myself away from Devlin, who was smoothing my hair with his hands. But presently I managed to scream:

"'Don't touch me! Don't touch me, you – you —'

"'You what?' asked Devlin in his false voice, moving a little away from my chair.

"My scream, and him speaking agin, brought me to myself.

"'Never mind, never mind,' I said. 'If you know what I'm thinking about, it's no use my telling you.'

"'I do know,' he said. 'Why, it's wrote on your face. And I know, too, that you want to ask me some questions. Fire away.'

"'Mr. Devlin, I said, upon that, 'you slep at home last night, didn't you?'

"'Certainly, I did,' he answered. 'Don't you remember Lemon and me coming in together?'

"'Yes,' I said, 'I remember.'

"'Don't you remember,' he said, 'that you brought me up a cup of tea before you went to bed, and that I told you I had a lot of writing to do, and that I said what a treasure you was, and how happy Lemon ought to be with sech a wife?'

"'Yes,' I said, 'I remember.' I couldn't say nothing else, it was the truth.

"'Inspired by the egsellent tea you make,' he went on, 'I stopped up late and did my writing. If I mistake not, you put the chain on the street-door before you went to bed.'

"'Yes, I did.'

"'And when you went down this morning the chain was still up?'

"'Yes, it was.'

"'And I breakfasted with you and Lemon?'

"'Yes, you did.'

"'And I presume you made my bed some time during the day?'

"'Of course I did.'

"'Did it look as if it had been slep in?'

"'Yes.'

"'So that you see, my dear landlady,' he said, grinning at me, 'that it wasn't possible for me to have murdered the girl.'

"'Who said you did it?' I asked, starting back, for he had come close to me, and I thought he was going to touch me ag'in.

"'You didn't say so,' he said, 'but you thought so. It was wrote in your face, as I told you a minute ago. It is women like you who would put a man's life in danger, and think no more of it than snuffing a candle.'

"He didn't remain with me much longer, but went up to his room. He was right in what he said he saw wrote in my face while he was smoothing my hair; an idea had entered my head that it was him who had killed the poor girl. I think him bad enough for anything; there's nothing wicked I wouldn't believe of him. But of course it wasn't possible for him to have done it; and I thought with thankfulness it wasn't possible for Lemon to have done it, for he never stirred out of the house that night. It was what Lemon said in his sleep that made me tremble and shiver. Why, sir, he spoke of the murder *before it was done!* It says in the papers that when the poor girl was found she had been dead hours, and the doctor fixes it that she must have been murdered between two and three o'clock in the morning. And two hours and a half before she was murdered Lemon was raving in his sleep and telling all about it! How did he know, sir? how did he know?

"If it had been a ordinary case – if Lemon had only spoke in his sleep about some murder or other, and I'd read the next day that a murder *had* been committed that night, it would have been strange, but nothing so very much out of the way. Our minds sometimes runs on dreadful things, enough to give one the creeps, and we ain't accountable for everything we say when we're asleep. But Lemon said Victoria Park, and it was done in Victoria Park. He said eighteen years, and that was jest her age. He said golden hair, and she *had* golden hair. He said a bunch of white daisies, and she wore a bunch of white daisies. He said blood on 'em, and there *was* blood on 'em. He said stabbed to the heart, and she *was* stabbed to the heart!

"I'll tell you, sir, what come to me, and made me feel almost like a murderess. It was that if I'd really known what was going to happen when I heard Lemon talking in his sleep, I might have saved the life of that poor girl. But how was it possible for me to know? Still, that didn't prevent me feeling like a guilty woman.

"But how much did Lemon know? Did the wretch who killed the girl tell him beforehand what he was going to do, and was Lemon wicked enough to keep it to hisself? Was the murderer an acquaintance of Lemon's? If he was, I made up my mind that a hour shouldn't pass after Lemon was awake this morning before I put the police on the wretch's track. Lemon would know his name, and where he lived, perhaps. Whatever was the consequences, I'd do what I could to bring the monster into the dock.

"I was more than sorry that the doctor had give Lemon sech a strong sleeping draught, and I prayed that he would wake up sooner than I expected. I went to the bedroom, but there was Lemon fast asleep, with a face as innocent as a babe unborn. He wasn't dreaming, he wasn't talking; his mind was at rest as well as his body. You know more than I do, sir. Could anybody with something dreadful on his mind have slep' like that? But my mind was made up. The very minute Lemon was sensible, and knew what he was about, to the police-station he should go with me, and make a clean breast of it."

XVI

MR. LEMON WAKES UP

"I was that impatient that I hardly knew what to do. Minutes was like dymens, and there Lemon lay like a log. Couldn't I bring him to his senses somehow or other? I tried. I walked about heavy. I threw down things. I even turned Lemon over, but it had no more effect on him than water on a duck's back. He never give so much as a murmur, and I don't think a earthquake would have roused him. I had to give it up as a bad job, but I felt that it would be a mockery for me to go to bed, because in the state I was in it wasn't likely I could git a wink of sleep. Then I knew, too, that there wouldn't be a minute to lose when Lemon opened his eyes, and that it was my duty to git everything ready. So I spread out Lemon's clothes in regular order, not forgetting his clean Sunday shirt, and I put on my bonnet and cloak, and set down and waited all through that blessed night, looking at Lemon. I didn't hear a sound in the room upstairs, so I supposed that Devlin was asleep, and I thought how dreadful it was to have a man like that in the house, a man as spoke of murder as though he enjoyed it. The only sound that come to my ears two or three times in the night was the policeman on his beat outside as he passed through the square, and you may guess, sir, I didn't get any comfort out of that. I had my fancies, but I shook 'em off, though they made me shake and shiver. One of 'em was that all of a sudden, jest as the policeman had passed by, there rung through the square shrieks of 'Murder! murder!' and millions of people seemed to be battering at the street-door and crying that they'd tear Lemon and me to pieces. It didn't seem as if they wanted to hurt Devlin, for there he was, standing and grinning at us and the people, with that aggravating look on his face that makes me burn to fly at him, if I only had the courage. Of course it was all fancy, sir; but how would you like to pass sech a night?

"At nine o'clock this morning, and not a minute before, Lemon woke up. I had a cup of tea ready for him in the bedroom, and a slice of bread and butter. He's gone off his breakfast for a long time past, and one slice of bread and butter is as much as he can git down, if he can do that. Before I took Devlin as a lodger, Lemon used to eat a big breakfast, never less than a couple of rashers, and a couple of boiled eggs on the top of that, and four or five slices of bread and butter cut thick. It is a bad sign when a man begins to say he's got no appetite for breakfast. If his stomach ain't going all to pieces, it's something worse, perhaps.

" 'Why, Fanny,' said Lemon, seeing me with my bonnet on, 'have you been out? What's the time?'

"He spoke quite calm and cheerful; the sleeping draught had done him good, and had made him forgit.

" 'The time's nine o'clock, Lemon,' I answered, 'and I ain't been out.'

" 'What's today?' he asked.

" 'Sunday,' I answered.

" 'Sunday!' he exclaimed. 'It's funny. Everything seems mixed. Sunday, is it? But, I say, Fanny, if you ain't been out, what have you got your bonnet on for?'

" 'I'm waiting for you,' I said. 'Git up, quick, you must come with me at once.'

"'Come with you at once,' he said, rubbing his eyes, to make sure whether he was awake or asleep; and then he must have seen something in my face, for he looked at me strange, and left off rubbing his eyes, and began to rub his forehead. 'I can't understand it. Has anything gone wrong?'

"'Lemon,' I said, speaking very solemn, and speaking as I felt, 'you know too well what has gone wrong, and I only hope you may be forgiven.'

"I shouldn't have stopped short in the middle if it hadn't been that we heard Devlin moving about in the room upstairs. I looked up at the ceiling, and so did Lemon, and when I saw his face grow white I knew that mine was growing white as well; and I knew, too, that Lemon was gitting his memory back.

"'Speak low, speak low,' he whispered. 'Devlin mustn't hear a word we say. You hope I may be forgiven! For what? What have I done? O, my head, my head! It feels as if it was going to burst!'

"His face begun to get flushed, and the veins swelled out. I thought to myself, I must be careful with Lemon; I mustn't be too sudden with him, or he'll have another fit. I was going to speak soothing, when he clapped his hand on my mouth and almost stopped my breath.

"'Don't say nothing yet,' he said. 'You must tell me something first that I want to know. I feel so confused – so confused! What's been the matter with me? I don't remember going to bed last night.'

"'You fell down in a fit, Lemon,' I said, 'and I had to get the doctor to you.'

"'Yes, yes,' he said eagerly. 'Go on – go on.'

"'We carried you upstairs here, the doctor and me, and undressed you and put you to bed; and when you come out of your fit he give you a sleeping draught.'

"'It's not that I want to know,' he said. 'What *made* me go into a fit? I never had a fit before, as I remember. O Fanny, is it all a dream?'

" 'Lemon,' I answered, 'you must ask your conscience; I can't answer you. You come home with a evening paper in your pocket, a-moaning and crying, and you ketches hold of me, and looks round as if a ghost had follered you into the room, and then you falls down in your fit.'

" 'And him?' he said, pointing to the ceiling. 'Him – Devlin? Was he with me? Did he see me while I was in the fit?'

" 'No,' I answered. 'He come home after we'd got you to bed, and said he wanted to see you; but I wouldn't let him. I whipped upstairs here, and turned the key, so as he shouldn't git at you.'

" 'You did right, you did right. Was he angry?'

" 'If he was, he didn't show it. He kep with me a long time, talking about the –the—'

" 'About the what?' asked Lemon, the perspiration breaking out on him.

" 'About the murder! Well may you shiver! It was in the newspaper you brought home with you, and he read it out loud, and talked about it in a way as froze my blood.'

" 'Blood!' groaned Lemon, 'Blood! O Fanny, Fanny!'

"He is my husband, sir, and he was suffering, and I ain't ashamed to say that I took him in my arms, and tried to comfort him.

" 'One word, Lemon,' I said, 'only one word before we go on. You ain't guilty, are you?'

" 'Guilty?' he answered, but speaking quite soft; we neither of us raised our voices above a whisper 'My God, no! How could I be? Wasn't I at home and abed when it was done? O, it's horrible! horrible! and I don't know what to think.'

" 'Thank God, you're innocent!' I said, and I was so grateful in my heart that my eyes brimmed over. 'And you didn't have nothing to do with the planning of it? Tell me that.'

" 'No, Fanny,' he said. '*Him* upstairs there – did *he* sleep at home last night?'

"'Unless there's something going on too awful to think of,' I said, 'he did. I ain't been in bed, Lemon, since home you come yesterday and had your fit. And here in this room I've been setting with you from the time I put the chain on the street-door last night till now. I've only left you once – to take in the milk at seven o'clock this morning, and then the chain was on; it hadn't been touched. No one went out of this house last night by the street-door.'

"'They couldn't have gone out no other way,' said Lemon.

"'I don't see how they could,' I said, though I had my thoughts.

"'And the night before, Fanny,' said Lemon, and now he looked at me as if life and death was in my answer, 'the night it was done, did he sleep at home then?'

"'To the best of my belief he did,' I said. 'You may put me on the rack and tear me with red hot pinchers, and I can't say nothing but the truth. He *did* sleep here the night that awful murder was done in Victoria Park. Drag me to the witness-box and put me in irons, and I can't say nothing else. I saw him go to his room after I'd put up the chain; he called out 'Good night;' and the next morning the chain was up jest as I left it. You can't put the chain on the street-door from the outside; it must be done from the in. And now, Lemon, listen to me.'

"'What do you want?' he groaned. 'O, what do you want? Ain't I bad enough already that you try to make me worse?'

"'I *must* say, Lemon, what is on my mind.'

"'Won't it keep, Fanny?' he asked.

"'It won't keep,' I answered. 'You know the man as committed the murder, and you'll come with me to the police-station, and put the police on his track.'

"'*Me* know the wretch!' Lemon cried, his eyes almost starting out of his head. 'Have you gone mad?'

"'No, Lemon,' I answered, 'I'm in my sober senses. Whatever happens afterwards, we've got to face the consequences, or we shall wake up in the middle of the night and see that poor girl standing at our bedside pointing her finger at us. It's no use trying to disguise it. I *know* you know the wretch, and deny it you shan't.'

"'O,' he said, speaking very slow, as if he was choosing words, 'you know I know him!'

"'I do,' I answered.

"'Perhaps,' he said, with something like a click in his throat, 'you will tell me how that's possible, when it's gospel truth I've never set eyes on him all my born days.'

"'Lemon,' I said, 'be careful, O, be careful, how you speak of gospel truth! Remember Ananias! You may beat about the bush as much as you like, but I'm determined to do what I've made up my mind to, and nothing shall drive me from it.'

"'Of course,' he said, upon that, and speaking flippant, 'if you've made up your mind to the egstent you speak of, I'd best shut my mouth. I'll keep it shut till you tell me how you know what you say you know.'

"'Lemon,' I said, 'light you speak, but sech you don't feel. You can't deceive me. When we was first married, you slep the sleep of innocence, and your breathing was that regular as showed you had nothing on your mind to take egsception to. But since that Devlin come into the house, the way you've gone on of a night is simply awful. Jumping about in bed as you've been doing night after night, and screaming and talking in your sleep—'

"'Talking in my sleep!' he cried, and I saw that I'd scared him. 'You shouldn't have let me! Call yourself a wife? You should have stopped me!'

"'I couldn't help letting you, and I couldn't have stopped you, Lemon, and I'm not sure whether it would have been right to do it if sech was in my power.'

"'What have I said, what have I said?' he asked.

"'The night before last as ever was,' I said, 'when that dreadful deed was done as was printed in the paper you brought home yesterday, you said, while you was laying asleep on the very bed you're laying on now, words as chilled my blood, and it's a mercy I'm alive to tell it. You spoke of Victoria Park; you spoke of a beautiful young girl with hair the colour of gold; you spoke – O, Lemon, Lemon! – you spoke of her being stabbed to the heart; you spoke of a bunch of white daisies as she wore in her belt, and you said there was blood on 'em—'

"I had to stop myself, sir; for Lemon had hid his face in the bedclothes, and was shaking like a man with Sam Witus's dance in his marrer. I let him lay till he got over it a bit, and then he uncovered his face; it was as white as a sheet.

"'Fanny,' he said – and he was hardly able to get his words out – 'there's the Bible on the mantel-shelf, there. Bring it to me.'"

XVII

LEMON'S VISION IN THE TWISTED COW

"I fetched the Bible, sir, and he took it in his hand, and swore a most solemn oath, and kissed the book on it, that he didn't know the man, that he didn't know the girl, and that he had no more to do with the murder than a babe unborn. Never in my life did I see a man in sech a state as he was.

"'But, Lemon,' I said, 'how could you come to speak sech words? How could you come to know all about the murder hours and hours before it was done?'

"'I'll tell you, Fanny,' he said, 'as fur as I know; and if you was to cut me in a thousand pieces I couldn't tell you more.'

"'It ain't to be egspected,' I said.

"'If there's men in the world,' Lemon went on, 'as can look into the future, Devlin's one of 'em. If there's men in the world as can tell you what's going to happen – without having anything to do with it theirselves, mind – Devlin's one of 'em. The things he's told me of people is unbelievable, but as true as true can be. "Did you take particular notice of the gentleman whose hair I've been jest cutting?" he said to me. "No," says I; "why should I?" "He's the great Mr. Danebury that all the world's talking of," says he. "Is he?" says I. "I wonder what brings him to our shop? What a charitable man he is! "What a good, good man he is!" "Good ain't the word for him," says Devlin. "He comes to our shop because it's out of the way. All the while I was operating on him he was thinking of a little milliner's girl as he's got an appointment with tonight. 'Pretty little Ph[oe]be!' he was saying to hisself as I was cutting his hair. 'What eyes she's got! Bloo and swimming! What a skin's she's got! like satting, it is so white and smooth! What lips she's got! She's a bit of spring, jest budding. Pritty little Ph[oe]be – pretty little Ph[oe]be!'" "But what was he saying that for?" I asks. "He can't be in love with her. He's a family man, ain't he?" "I should think he was a family man," says Devlin. "He's got the most beautiful wife a man could wish for, and as good as she's beautiful; and he's got half-a-dozen blooming children. But that don't prevent his being in love with pritty little Ph[oe]be, and he's got an appointment with her tonight; and, what's more, he's going to keep it." I'm putting a true case to you, Fanny,' says Lemon, 'one of many sech. I fires up at what Devlin says about such a good man – that is, I used to fire up when things first commenced. I don't dispute with him now; I know it's no use, and that he's always right, and me always wrong. But then I did, and I asks him how dare he talk like that of sech a man as Mr. Danebury, as gives money to charities, and talks about being everybody's friend. "O, you don't believe me!" Devlin says. "Well, come with me tonight, and we'll jest see for ourselves." And I go with him, and I see a pritty little girl walking up and down the dark turning at the bottom of the Langham Hotel. Up and down she walks, up and down, up and down. "That must be her," says Devlin. We keep watching a little way off on the other side of the way, where it's darker still than where she's walking and waiting, and presently who should come up to her but the great Mr. Danebury; and he takes her hand and holds it long, and they stand talking, and he says something to make her laugh, and then he tucks her arm in his, and walks off with her. "What do you think of that?" Devlin asks. "He's going to take her to a meeting of the missionary society." What I think of it makes me melancholy, and makes me ask myself, "Can sech things be?" At another time Devlin says, "I shouldn't wonder if you heard of a big fire tomorrer." "Why do you say that?" I asks. "The man who's jest gone out," Devlin answers, "was thinking of one while I was shampooing him – that's all." And that *was* all; but sure enough I do read of a big fire tomorrer in a great place of business that's heavily insured, and there's lives lost and dreadful scenes. And then sometimes when Devlin and me is setting together, he gits up all of a sudden and stands over me, and what he does to me I couldn't tell you if you was to burn me alive; but my senses seems to go, and I either gits fancies, or Devlin puts 'em in my head; but when I come to there's Devlin setting before me, and he says, "I'll wager," says he, "that I'll tell you what you've been dreaming of." "Have I been asleep?" I asks. "Sound," he answers, "and talking in your sleep." And he tells me something dreadful that I've said about something that's going to happen; and before the week's out it does happen, and I read of it in the papers. For a long time this has been going on till I've got in that state that I'd as soon die as live. If you don't understand what I'm trying to egsplain, Fanny,' said my poor Lemon, 'it ain't my fault; it's as dark to me as it is to you. Sometimes I says to Devlin, "I'll go and warn the police." "Do," says Devlin, "and be took up as a accomplice, and be follered about all your life like a thief or a murderer. Go and tell, and git yourself hanged or clapped in a madhouse." Of course, I see the sense of that, and I keep my mouth shut, but I get miserabler and miserabler. So the day before yesterday –that's Friday, Fanny – Devlin and me is sitting in the private room of the Twisted Cow, when he asks me whether I've ever been to Victoria Park, and I answers "Lots of times." Now Fanny,' said Lemon, breaking off in his awful confession, 'if you ain't prepared to believe what's coming, I'll say no more. It'll sound unbelievable, but I can't help that. Things has happened without me having anything to do with 'em, and I'd need to be a sperrit instead of a man to account for 'em.'

"'Lemon,' I said, 'I'm prepared to believe everything, only don't keep nothing from me.'

"'I won't,' said Lemon; 'I'll tell you as near and as straight as I can what happened after Devlin asked me whether I'd ever been to Victoria Park. His eyes was fixed upon me that strange that I felt my senses slipping away from me; it wasn't that things went round so much as they seemed to fade away and become nothing at all. Was I setting in the private room of the Twisted Cow? I don't know. Was it day or night? I don't know. I wouldn't swear to it, though the moon *was* shining through the trees. The trees where? Why, in Victoria Park, and no place else. And there was a man and a woman – a young beautiful woman, with golden hair, and a bunch of white daisies in her belt – talking together. How do I know that she's young and beautiful when I didn't see her face? That's one of the things I'm unable to answer. And I don't see the man's face, either. Whether a minute passed or a hour, before I heard a shriek, I can't say, and perhaps it ain't material. And upon the shriek, there, near the water, laid the young girl, dead, with the bunch of white daisies in her belt, stained with blood. Then, everything disappeared, and, trembling and shaking to that degree that I felt as if I must fall to pieces, I looked up and round, and found myself in the private room of the Twisted Cow, with Devlin setting opposite me. "Dreaming agin, Lemon?" he says, with a grin. But I don't answer him; my tongue sticks to the roof of my mouth. That's all I know, Fanny. Whether I saw what I've told you, or was told it, or only fancied it, is beyond me. What I've said is the truth, the whole truth, and nothing but the truth, so help me God!'

"That's what I heard from Lemon's own lips this morning, sir, up-stairs, abed, where he is laying now, with the door locked on him.

"I took off my hat and cloak, and Lemon burst out crying.

" 'You believe me, Fanny!' he cried.

" 'I believe every word you said,' I answered. 'It's no use going to the police-station this morning. A good friend of our'n is coming to see me today, and we'll wait and do what he advises us. Only you must promise to see him.' And I told him who you was, and why I wrote to you on Friday before poor Lizzie Melladew met her death.

" 'I promise,' said Lemon, 'and you've done right, Fanny.'

"And now, sir, I've told you everything as I said I would, and you know as much as I do about this dreadful business."

XVIII

FANNY'S STORY BEING CONCLUDED, I PAY A VISIT TO MR. LEMON, AND RESOLVE TO INTERVIEW DEVLIN THE BARBER

This was the story which Fanny related to me, and to which I listened in wonder and amazement. As she related it I wondered at times whether it was possible that what she said could be true, but I saw no reason to question her veracity; and there certainly could be no doubt of her sincerity. I had to some extent conquered the fascination which Lemon's portrait on the wall, the stuffed bird in its glass case, and the evil-looking monster on the mantelshelf had exercised over me, but even now I could scarcely gaze upon them without a shudder. Fanny did not relate her story straight off, without a break, and I need hardly say that it was much longer than is here transcribed. But I have omitted no important point; everything pertinent to the tragedy of the murder of Mr. Melladew's daughter is faithfully set down. When she finished it was quite dark; at my request she had not lighted lamp or candle.

There were breaks, as I have said. Twice she left off, and went up-stairs to see Lemon, and give him something to eat and drink.

"He knows you're here, sir," she said, when she returned on the first occasion.

"Is he impatient to see me?" I asked.

"No, sir," she replied. "All he seems to want is to be left alone."

"But he will see me?"

"O, yes, sir! He'll keep his promise."

Once there was an interval of more than half-an-hour, during which I ate some cold meat and bread she brought me, and drank a pint bottle of stout.

There was another occasion when she suddenly paused, with her finger at her lips.

"What are you stopping for, Fanny?" I asked.

"Speak low, sir," she said. "Devlin!"

"Where?" I said, much startled.

"He has just opened the street-door, sir."

"I heard nothing, Fanny."

"No, sir, you wouldn't. You don't know his ways as I do. Don't speak for a minute or two, sir."

I waited, and strained my ears, but no footfall reached my ears. Presently Fanny said:

"He's gone up to his room. He waited outside Lemon's door, and tried it, I think. Have you any notion what you are going to do about him, sir?"

"My ideas are not yet formed, but I intend to see and speak with him."

"You do, sir?"

"I do, Fanny, A special providence has directed my steps here today. I knew the poor girl who has been murdered."

"Sir!"

"Her family and mine have been friends for years. The interest I take in the discovery of the murderer is no common interest, and I intend to bring him to justice."

"How, sir?" exclaimed Fanny, greatly excited.

"Through Mr. Devlin. The way will suggest itself. You have not heard him leave the house since he entered a little while since?"

"No, sir. He is in his room now."

"If," I said, "when I am with your husband – and I intend to remain with him but a short time – Devlin comes downstairs, let me know immediately. Keep watch for him."

"I will, sir. O, how thankful I am that you're here – how thankful, how thankful!"

"I hope we shall all have reason to be thankful. And now, Fanny, I will go up to your husband."

"I'll go in first, and prepare him, sir."

"Let us have lights in the house. Don't leave Mr. Lemon in the dark. Put a candle in the passage also."

She followed my instructions, and then we went to her husband's bedroom. I waited outside while she "prepared" him. It did not take long to do so, and she came to the door and beckoned to me. I entered the room, and desired her to leave us alone.

"But don't lock us in," I added.

"No, sir," she said. "Lemon's safe now you're with him."

With that she retired, first smoothing the bedclothes and the pillow with a kind of pitying, soothing motion as though Lemon was about to undergo an operation.

I moved the candle so that its light fell upon Lemon's face. A scared, frightened face it was that turned towards me, the face of a man who had received a deadly shock.

It is unnecessary to say more than a few words about what passed between Mr. Lemon and myself. My purpose was to obtain from him confirmation of the strange mysterious story which Fanny had related. In this purpose I succeeded; it was correct in every particular. What I elicited from Lemon was elicited in the form of questions which I put to him and which he answered, sometimes readily, sometimes reluctantly. Had time not been so precious, my curiosity would have impelled me to go into matters respecting Devlin other than the murder of Lizzie Melladew, but I felt there was not a minute to waste; and at the termination of my interview with Lemon I went into the passage, where I found Fanny waiting for me. Whispering to her not to remain there, in order that Devlin might not be too strongly prejudiced against me – supposing him to be on the watch as well as ourselves – and receiving from her instructions as to the position of his room, I mounted the stairs with a firm, loud tread, and stood in the dark at the door which was to conduct me to the presence of the mysterious being.

XIX

FACE TO FACE WITH DEVLIN, I DEMAND AN EXPLANATION OF HIM

I rapped with my knuckles, and a voice which could have been none other than the voice of Devlin immediately responded, calling to me to enter. The next moment I stood face to face with the strange creature, concerning whom my curiosity was raised to the highest pitch. He was sitting in a chair upon my entrance, and he did not rise from it; therefore I looked down upon him and he looked up at me. As my eyes rested on his face, I saw in it the inspiration of the evil expression in the faces of Mr. Lemon's portrait, the stone monster, and the bird's beak, which had made so profound an impression upon me in the parlour on the ground-floor.

"You have been in the house some time," said Devlin.

"I have," I answered.

"And have had a long, a very long, conversation with my worthy landlady," he observed.

"Yes," I said.

"About me," he said, not in the form of a question but as a statement of fact.

"Partly about you."

"And about poor Lemon?"

"Yes, about him as well."

"Sit down," said Devlin, "I expected you."

There was only one other chair in the room besides the one he occupied, and I accepted his invitation, and drew it up to the table. And there we sat gazing at each other for what appeared to me a long time in silence.

The room was very poorly furnished. There were the two chairs, a small deal table, and a single iron bedstead in the corner. Off the room was a kind of closet, in which I supposed were a washstand and fittings. There was only one other article in view in addition to those I have mentioned, and that was a desk at which Devlin was writing. He did not put away his papers, and I was enabled to observe, without undue prying, that his writing was very fine and very close.

How shall I describe him? A casual observation of his face and figure would not suffice for the detection of anything uncanny about him, but it must be remembered that I was abnormally excited, and most strangely interested in him. He was tall and dark, his face was long and spare; his forehead was low; his eyes were black, with an extraordinary brilliancy in them; his mouth was large, and his lips thin. He wore a moustache, but no beard. In the order and importance of the impressions they produced upon me I should place first, his black eyes with their extraordinary brilliancy, and next, his hands, which were unusually small and white. They were the hands of a lady of gentle culture rather than those of a man in the class of life to which Devlin appeared to belong. Not alone was his social standing presumably fixed by the fact of his living in a room so poorly furnished at the top of a house so common as Mr. Lemon's, but his clothes were a special indication. They were shabby and worn; black frock-coat, black trousers and waistcoat, narrow black tie. Not a vestige of colour about them, and no sign of jewellery of any kind.

"Well?" he said.

I started. I had been so absorbed in my observance of him that I, who should have been the first to plunge into the conversation, had remained silent for a time so unreasonably long that the man upon whom I had intruded might have justly taken offence.

"I beg your pardon," I said; "did you not remark that you expected me?"

"Yes."

"May I inquire upon what grounds your expectation was based?"

He smiled; and here I observed, in the quality of this smile, a characteristic of which Mrs. Lemon had given me no indication. Devlin was evidently gifted with a touch of humour.

"I reason by analogy," he said. "My landlady has very few visitors. You are here for the first time, with an object. You remain closeted with her for hours. She probably sent for you. During the long interview downstairs you have been told a great deal about me. You hear me open the street-door, and you know I am in the house. My landlady has a trouble on her mind, and mixes me up with it. You have been made acquainted with this trouble and with my supposed connection with it. Your curiosity has been aroused, and you determine to seek an interview with me before you take your leave of her. You come up uninvited, and here you are, as I expected. Am I logical?"

"Quite logical."

"In a common-sense view of commonplace matters – and everything in the world is commonplace – lies the ripest wisdom. Follow my example. Exercise your common sense."

But I did not immediately speak. Devlin's words were so different from what I had expected that I was for a moment at a loss. The prospect of my being able to bring the murderer of Lizzie Melladew to justice and of earning a thousand pounds did not appear so bright.

"I will assist you," he resumed; "I will endeavour to set you at your ease with me. Your scrutiny of me has been very searching; I ought to feel flattered. What anticipations of my appearance you may have entertained before you entered the room is your affair, not mine. How far they are realised is your affair, not mine. But allow me to assure you, my dear sir," and here he rose to his full height, and made me a half-humorous, half-mocking bow, "that I am a very ordinary person."

"That cannot be," I said, "after what I have heard."

"It is the destiny," he said, resuming his seat, "of greater personages than myself to be ranked much higher than they deserve. Proceed."

"I am here to speak to you about this murder," I said, plunging boldly into the subject.

"Ah, about a murder! But there are so many."

"You know to which one I refer. The murder of a young girl in Victoria Park, which took place the night before last."

"I have heard and read of it," said Devlin.

"You know also," I continued, "that the tragedy has produced in Mr. Lemon a condition of mind and body which may lead to dangerous results, probably to a despairing death."

"All men must die," he said cynically.

I was now thoroughly aroused. "I have come to you for an explanation," I said, "and it must be a satisfactory one."

"You speak like an inquisitor," said Devlin, with a quiet smile, and I seemed to detect in his altered manner a desire to irritate me and to drive me into an excess of passion. For this reason I kept myself cool, and simply said,

"I am resolved."

"Good. Keep resolved."

"I shall do so. By some devilish and mysterious means you were aware, before the poor girl left her home on Friday night, that her doom was sealed. You could have prevented it, and you did not raise a hand to save her. This knowledge I have gained from Mr. Lemon, to whom, through you, the impending tragedy was known."

"Then why did *he* not prevent it?"

"It was not in his power. He was not acquainted with the names of the murderer and his victim."

"Was I?"

"You must have been. I do not pretend to an understanding of the extraordinary power you exercise, but I am convinced that, in connection with you, there is a mystery which should be brought to light, and if I can be the agent to unmask you I am ready for the work. With all the earnestness of my soul, I swear it."

A low laugh escaped Devlin's lips. "Were a commissioner of lunacy here," he said, "you would be in peril. This young girl you speak of, is she in any way connected with you?"

"She was my friend; I knew her from childhood; she has sat at my table with her sister and parents, and I and mine have sat at theirs. Her family are plunged into the lowest depths of despair by the cruel, remorseless blow which has fallen upon them."

"And you have taken upon yourself the task of an avenger. It is chivalrous, but is it entirely unselfish? I am always suspicious of mere words; there is ever behind them a secret motive, hidden by a dark curtain. I speak in metaphor, but you will seize my meaning, for you are a man of nerve and intelligence, utterly unlike our friend in the room below, whose nature is servile and abject, and who is not, as you are, given to heroics. Calm yourself. I am ready to discuss this matter with you, but in your present condition I should have the advantage of you. You are heated; I am cool and collected. You have some self-interest at heart; I have none. Your words are so wild that any person but myself hearing them would take you for a madman. For your own sake – not for mine, for the affair does not concern me – I advise moderation of language. I suppose you will scarcely believe that the man upon whom you have unceremoniously intruded, and against whom you launch accusations, the very extravagance of which renders them unworthy of serious consideration – you will scarcely believe that this man is simply a poor barber who has not a second coat to his back, nor a second pair of shoes to his feet. But it is a fact – a proof of the injustice of the world, ever blind to merit. For I am not only a barber, sir, I am a capable workman, as I will convince you. Pray do not move; a cooling essence and a brush skilfully used effect wonders on an over-heated head."

It was not in my power to resist him. He had taken his place behind my chair, and before he had finished speaking had sprinkled a liquid over my head which was so overpoweringly refreshing that I insensibly yielded to its influence. With brush and comb he arranged my hair, his small white hands occasionally touching my forehead gently and persuasively. When I thought afterwards of this strange incident I called to mind that, for the two or three minutes during which he was engaged in the exercise of his art, I was in a kind of quiet dream, in which all the agitating occurrences of the previous day in connection with the murder of Lizzie Melladew were mentally repeated in proper sequence, closing with Mr. Portland's offer of a thousand pounds for the discovery of the murderer. It was, as it were, a kind of panorama which passed before me of all that occurred between morning and night. I looked up, inexpressibly refreshed, and with my mind bright and clear. Devlin stood before me, smiling.

"Confess, sir," he said, in a soft persuasive tone, "that I have returned good for evil. The fever of the brain is abated, or I am a bungler indeed. We will now discuss the matter."

XX

DEVLIN ASTONISHES ME

"I remarked to you just now," he said, seating himself comfortably in his chair, "that I am always suspicious of mere words, for the reason that there is ever a secret motive behind them. From what you have said I should be justified in supposing that your desire to discover the mystery in which the death of your poor young friend is involved springs simply from sympathy with her bereaved family. I will not set a trap for you, and pin you to that statement by asking questions which you would answer only in one way. You would argue with yourself probably as to the disingenuousness of those answers, but would finally appease your conscience by deciding that I, a perfect stranger to you and your affairs, cannot possibly have anything to do with the private motives by which you are influenced. Say, for instance, by such a motive as the earning of a reward which we will put down at a thousand pounds."

For the life of me I could not restrain a start of astonishment. It was the exact sum Mr. Portland had offered me. By what dark means had Devlin divined it?

"You need not be discomposed," said Devlin. "The thing is natural enough. You have credited me with so much that it will harm neither of us if you credit me with a little more – say, with a certain faculty for reading men's thoughts. The world knows very little as yet; it has much to learn; and I, in my humble way, may be a master in a new species of spiritual power. Now, I have a profound belief in Fate; what it wills must inevitably be. And, impressed by this article of faith, I, the master, may be willing to become the slave. Fate has led you to this house, and it may be that you are an instrument in discoveries yet to be made. I continue, you observe, to speak occasionally in metaphor. Be as frank with me as I have been with you. No, don't trouble yourself to speak immediately. In the words you were about to utter there is a subterfuge; you have not yet made up your mind to be entirely open with me. You and I meet now for the first time. Before this day I have never known of your existence, nor have you been aware of mine."

"If that be true," I said, interrupting him, "what made you mention the reward of a specific sum?"

"Of a thousand pounds?" he asked, smiling.

"Exactly."

"Do you deny that such a reward has been offered to you?"

"I do not deny it; but by what mysterious means did you come to the knowledge of it?"

"Because it is in your mind, my dear sir," he said.

"That is no answer."

"Is it not? I should have thought it would satisfy you, but you are inclined to be unreasonable. Come, now, I will show you how little I am concealing from you with respect to my knowledge of your movements." He shaded his eyes with his hand, and looked at me from beneath it.

"I do not know your name, nor in what part of London you reside, but certainly you and your wife – no doubt a most estimable lady – were sitting together at breakfast yesterday morning."

He paused, and waited for me to speak. "It is quite true," I said; "but there is nothing unusual in husband and wife partaking of that meal in company."

"Nothing in the least unusual if a man is master of his own time, as you were yesterday morning, for the first time for a long while past. The fact is, you had lost a situation in which you have been employed for years."

I sat spellbound. Devlin continued:

"The breakfast-things are on the table, and you and your lady are discussing ways and means. You are not rich, and you look forward with some fear to the future. Times are hard, and situations are not easy to obtain. In the midst of your consultation a man rushes into the room. He is a middle-aged man. Shall I describe him?"

"If you can," I said, my wonder growing.

He gave me a fairly faithful description of Mr. Melladew, and proceeded:

"A great grief has fallen upon this man. It is only within the last hour that he has discovered that his daughter had been murdered. He remains with you some time, and then other persons make their appearance, among them newspaper reporters and policemen, all doubtless drawn to your house by this business of the murder. You have also an interview with a young gentleman. The day passes. It is evening, and you are seated with another person. By this person you are offered one thousand pounds if you discover the murderer of the young girl, and another thousand if you find her sister, who has strangely disappeared. I do not wish to deprive you of such credit as belongs to a man who sympathises with a friend in trouble; but it is certainly a fact that the dim prospect of earning such a handsome sum of money is very strong within you. That is all."

I deliberated awhile in silence, and Devlin did not disturb my musings. All that he had narrated had passed through my mind while he was engaged in dressing my hair. Had he the power of reading thoughts by the mere action of his fingers upon a man's head? No other solution occurred to me, and had I not been placed in my present position I should instantly have rejected it; but now I was in the mood for entertaining it, wild and incredible as it appeared. During this interval of silence I made a strong endeavour to calm myself for what was yet to take place between me and Devlin, and I was successful. When I spoke I was more composed.

"You say you do not know where I live. Is it true?" I asked.

"Quite true," he answered.

"You do not really know my name?"

"I do not."

"Nor the names of my visitors?"

"Nor the names of your visitors."

"But you must be aware," I said, "admitting, for the sake of argument, that you are not romancing—"

"Yes," he said, laughing, "admitting that, for the sake of argument."

"You must be aware that the name of the first man who visited me – he being, as you have declared, the father of the murdered girl – is Melladew."

"I am aware of it, not from actual knowledge, but from what I have read in the newspapers."

"But of the name of the gentleman who, you say, offers the reward of a thousand pounds, you are ignorant."

"Quite ignorant. Now, having replied to your questions frankly, confess that you have forced yourself upon me with a distinct motive, in which I, a stranger to you, am interested."

"My object is to discover the murderer and bring him to justice."

"A very estimable design."

"And also to discover what has become of the murdered girl's sister."

"Exactly. How do you propose to accomplish your object?"

"Through you."

"Indeed! Through me?"

"As surely as we are in the same room together, through you. Receive what I am about to say as the fixed resolve of a man who sees before him a stern duty and will not flinch from it. Having come into association with you, I am determined not to lose sight of you. I put aside any further consideration of a strange and inexplicable mystery in connection with yourself as being utterly and entirely beyond my power to understand."

"My dear sir," said Devlin, with a glance at his shabby clothes, "you flatter me."

"All my energies now are bent to one purpose, which, through you, I shall carry to its certain end. You have made yourself plain to me. I hope up to this point I have made myself plain to you."

"You are the soul of lucidity," said Devlin, "but much remains yet to explain. For the sake of argument we have admitted an element of romance into this very prosaic matter; for it is really prosaic, almost commonplace. Life is largely made up of tragedies and mysteries, the majority of them petty and contemptible, a few only deserving to be called grand. As a matter of fact, my dear sir, existence, with all its worries, anxieties, hopes, and disappointments, is nothing better than a game of pins and needles. It is the littleness of human nature that magnifies a pin prick into a wound of serious importance. To think that some of these mortals should call themselves philosophers! It is laughable. Do you follow me?"

"Not entirely," I replied, "but I have some small glimmering of your meaning."

"Were your mind," said Devlin, shaking with internal laughter, "quite free from the influence of that thousand pounds, it would be clearer. In the grand Scheme of Nature, so far as mortals comprehend it, the potent screw is human selfishness. These speculations, however, are perhaps foreign to the point. Let us continue our amicable argument until we thoroughly understand each other upon the subject of this murder. You see, my dear sir, I wish to know exactly how I stand; for despite the extraordinary opinion you have formed of me, it is you who have assumed the *rôle* of Controller of Destinies. I am but a mere instrument in your hands." He measured me with his eyes. "You are well built, and are, I should judge, a powerful man."

"You are contemplating the probability of a physical struggle between us," I said. "Dismiss it; there will be none."

He made me a mocking bow. "My mind is, indeed, relieved. You do not intend violence, then. I am free to leave the house if I wish – at this moment, if I please. Have you taken that contingency into account?"

"I have."

"You will not attempt to detain me by force?"

"No."

"In such an event, how will you act?"

"I shall follow you, and to the first policeman I meet I shall say, 'Arrest that person. He is implicated in the murder of Lizzie Melladew.'"

Devlin cast upon me a look of admiration. "That would be awkward," he said.

"Decidedly awkward – for you."

"You would be asked to furnish evidence."

"Direct evidence it would be, at present, out of my power to supply," I said; I was on my mettle; my mental forces were never clearer, were never more resolutely set upon one object; "but there is such a thing as circumstantial evidence. Mr. Lemon and his wife should come forward, and relate all that they know concerning you. You and Mr. Lemon are carrying on a business somewhere; the place should be searched; it should be made food for the multitude who are ever on the hunt for the sensational. Your desk on the table here contains writings of yours; they may throw light upon the investigation. So we should go on, step by step, independent of your assistance, until we get the murderer – who may or may not be an accomplice of yours – into the clutches of the law."

Towards the end of this speech I had risen and approached the window, which faced the square. Mechanically lifting the blind, I looked out, and saw what arrested my attention. By the railings on the opposite side, with his eyes raised to the window, was the figure of a man. He was standing quite motionless, and, the night being fine, with a panoply of stars in the sky, I presently recognised the figure to be that of George Carton, poor Lizzie Melladew's distracted lover. At some little distance from him was the figure of another man, whose movements were distinguished by restlessness, and in him I recognised Carton's guardian, Mr. Kenneth Dowsett.

"Looking for a policeman?" inquired Devlin, with a touch of amusement in his voice.

"No," I replied, "but I am pleased to discover that I am not alone, that I have friends outside ready to assist me the moment I call upon them."

Devlin rose, and joined me at the window.

"Is your sight very keen?" he asked.

"Keen enough to recognise friends," I said.

"Mine is wonderful," said Devlin, "quite catlike; another of my abnormal qualities. I can plainly distinguish the features of the two men upon whom we are gazing. One is young. Who is he?"

"His name," I replied, believing that entire frankness would be more likely to win Devlin to my side, "is George Carton."

"I recognise him; he was in your house yesterday morning. He seems distressed. There is a troubled look in his face."

"He was the murdered girl's lover."

"Ah! And the other, the elder man, casting anxious glances upon the younger –who may he be?"

"His name is Mr. Kenneth Dowsett. He is young Carton's guardian."

"Thank you," said Devlin, returning to his seat at the table. I dropped the blind, and resumed my seat opposite to him, and then I observed a singular smile upon his face, to which I could attach no meaning.

"I presented," he said, "a certain contingency to you, the contingency of my leaving this house, and you have been delightfully explicit as to the course you would pursue. But, my dear sir, crediting myself with a species of occult power, which you appear ready to grant to me, might it not be in my power to vanish, to disappear from your sight the moment the policeman you would summons attempted to lay hands upon me?"

"I must chance that," I said.

"Good. Nothing of the sort will occur, I promise. I cannot carry on my pursuit as a Shadow. The idea of leaving the house did occur to me; I banish it. Well, then, suppose I remain here; suppose I put an end to this discussion; suppose I go to bed. To all your vapourings, suppose I say, 'Go to the devil!' Why on earth do you stare at me so? It is a common saying, and the awful consequences of such a journey are seldom thought of. I repeat, I say to you, 'Go to the devil!' What, then?"

"I still could summon a policeman," I said; "but even if I postponed that step or you managed to escape from me, I have a talent which, now that it occurs to me, I shall immediately press into my service."

"Enlighten me."

I took from my pocket some letters, and tore from them three blank leaves, upon which I set to work with pencil. My task occupied me ten minutes and more, during which time Devlin, sitting back in his chair, watched me with an expression of intense amusement in his face. When I had finished I handed him one of the blank leaves.

"My portrait!" he exclaimed. "I am an artist myself, as you have seen in Mrs. Lemon's parlour. This picture is the very image of me!"

"There is no mistaking it," I said complacently. "It will insure recognition."

"In what way do you propose to turn it to advantage, in the event of my being contumacious?"

"You have doubtless," I said, "noted the changes that have taken place in the life of civilised cities?"

"Excellent," he said. "My dear sir, you compel my admiration; you are altogether so different a person from the simpleton who lies shaking in his bed on the floor below. You have brain power. My worthy landlord and partner would have as well fulfilled his destiny had he been a mouse. The changes that have taken place! Ah, what changes have I not seen, say, in the course of the last thousand years!" And here he laughed loud and long. "But proceed, my dear sir, proceed. How do these changes affect me in the matter we are now considering?"

"There was a time—"

"Really, like the beginning of a fairy story," he interposed.

"When public opinion was of small weight, whereas now it is the most important factor in social affairs."

"Lucidly put. I listen to you with interest."

"The penny newspaper," I observed sagely, "is a mighty engine."

"You speak with the wisdom of a platitudinarian."

"It enlists itself in the cause of justice, and frequently plays, to a serviceable end, the part of a detective. You may remember the case of Leroy."

"A poor bungler, a very poor bungler. A small mind, my dear sir, eaten up by self-conceit of the lowest and meanest quality."

"For a long time Leroy evaded justice, but at length he was arrested. A popular newspaper published in its columns a portrait of the wretch—"

"I see," said Devlin, "and you would publish my portrait in the newspapers?"

"In every paper that would give it admittance; and few would refuse. Beneath it should be words to the effect that it was the portrait of a man who knew, before its committal, that the murder of the poor girl Lizzie Melladew was planned, and who must, therefore, be implicated in it. The portrait would lead to your arrest, and then Mr. and Mrs. Lemon would come forward with certain facts. Mr. Devlin, I would make London too hot to hold you."

"An expressive phrase. Your plan is more than ordinarily clever; it is ingenious. And London," said Devlin thoughtfully, "is such a place to work in, such a place to live in, such a place to observe in! To be banished from it would be a great misfortune. What other city in the world is so full of devilment and crime; what other city in the world is so full of revelations; what other city in the world is so full of opportunities, so full of contrasts, so full of hypocrisy and frivolity, so full of cold-blooded villainy? The gutters, with their ripening harvests of vice for gaol find gallows; the perfumed gardens, the fevered courts; the river, with its burden of jewels and beauty, with its burden of woe and despair; the bridges, with their nightly load of hunger, sin, and shame; the mansions, with their music, and false smiles, and aching hearts; the garrets, with their dim lights flickering; the bells, with their solemn warning; the busy streets, with their scheming life; the smug faces, the pinched bellies, the satins, the rags, the social treacheries, the suicides, the secret crimes, the rotting souls! My dear sir, the prospect of your making such a field too hot to hold even such a poor tatterdemalion as myself overwhelms me. What is the alternative?"

"That you pledge yourself by all that is holy and sacred to give me your fullest assistance towards the discovery of Lizzie Melladew's murderer."

XXI

DEVLIN AND I MAKE A COMPACT

"A sacred and holy pledge," said Devlin, "from me? Is it possible that you ask *me* to bind myself to you by a pledge that you deem holy and sacred?"

"I know of no other way to secure your assistance," I said, feeling the weight of the sneer.

"If you did, you would adopt it?"

"Assuredly."

"So that, after all, you are to a certain extent in my power."

"As you to a certain extent are in mine."

"A fair retort. Before I point out to you how illogical and inconsistent you are, let me thank you for having converted what promised to be a dull evening into a veritable entertainment. It is a real cause for gratitude in such a house as Lemon's, of whom I have already spoken disparagingly, but of whom I cannot speak disparagingly enough. My dear sir, that person is devoid of colour, his moral and physical qualities are feeble, his intellect may be said to be washed out. It is the bold, the daring, that recommends itself to me, although I admit that there are curious studies to be found among the meanest of mortals. Now, my dear sir, for your inconsistency and your lack of the logical quality. My worthy landlady has conveyed to you an impression of me which, to describe it truthfully, may be designated unearthly. How much farther it goes I will not inquire. Her small capacity has instilled into what, as a compliment, I will call her mind, a belief that I am not exactly human – in point of fact, that if I am not the Evil One himself, I am at least one of his satellites. Common people are inclined to such extravagances. They believe in apparitions, vampires, and supernatural signs, or, to speak more correctly, in signs which they believe to be supernatural. The most ordinary coincidences – and think, my dear sir, that there are myriads of circumstances, of more or less importance, occurring every twenty-four hours in this motley world, and that it is a mathematical certainty that a certain proportion of these myriads should be coeval and should bear some relation to each other – the most ordinary coincidences, I repeat, are outrageously magnified by their imaginations when, say, sickness or death is concerned. A woman wakes up in the night, and in the darkness hears a ticking – tick, tick, tick! She rises in the morning, and hears that her mother-in-law has died during the night. 'Bless my soul!' she exclaims. 'I knew it, I knew it! Last night I woke up all of a tremble' – (which, she did not, but that is a detail) – 'and heard the death-tick!' The story, being told to the neighbours, invests this woman, who is proud of having received a supernatural warning, with supreme importance. She becomes for a time a social star. She relates the story again and again, and each time adds something which her imagination supplies, until, in the end, it is settled that her mother-in-law died at the precise moment she woke up; that she saw the ghost of that person at her bedside, very ghastly and sulphury, in the moonlight – (it is always moonlight on these occasions) – that the ghost whispered in sepulchral tones, 'I am dying, goodbye;' that there was a long wail; and that then she jumped out of bed and screamed, 'My mother-in-law is dead!' This is the story after it has grown. What are the facts? The woman has eaten a heavy supper, and she sleeps not so well as usual; she wakes up in the middle of the night. In the kitchen a mouse creeps on to the dresser, after some crumbs of bread and cheese which are in a plate. The ever-watchful cat – I love cats, especially good mousers – jumps upon the dresser, with the intention of making a meal of the mouse. On the dresser, then, at this precise moment, are the plate containing the crumbs of bread and cheese, the mouse, and the cat. There are other things there, of course, but there is only one other thing connected with the story, and that is a jug half-full of water. The cat, jumping after the mouse, overturns this jug, and the water flows till it reaches the edge of the dresser, whence it drips, drips, drips, upon the floor. This is the tick, tick, tick which the woman upstairs hears – the death-tick of her mother-in-law! Her mother-in-law is eighty-seven years of age, and has been ill for months; her death is daily expected. She dies on this night, and the story is complete. A dying old woman, eighty-seven years of age, her daughter-in-law who has eaten too much supper, a plate of crumbs, a jug with water in it, a cat, and a mouse. Of these simple materials is a message from the unseen world created, which enthrals the entire neighbourhood. Analyse the miracles handed down from ancient times, some of which are woven into the religious beliefs of the people, and you will find that they are composed of parts as common and vulgar."

I made no attempt to interrupt Devlin in his narration of this commonplace story. He had, when he chose to exercise it, a singularly fascinating manner, and his voice was melodious, and when he paused I felt as if I had been listening to an attractive romance. While he spoke, his fingers were playing with a penholder and a pencil which were on the table; the penholder was long, the pencil was short, and I observed that he had placed one upon the other in the form of a cross.

"I am dull, perhaps," I said, "but I do not see how your story proves me to be illogical and inconsistent."

"I related it," replied Devlin, looking at the cross, "simply to show how willing people are to believe in the supernatural. My worthy landlady believes that I am a supernatural being; her husband believes it; *you* are inclined to lend a ready ear to it. And yet you tell me that you will be satisfied with a sacred and holy pledge from me, knowing, if you are at all correct in your estimate of me, that such a pledge is of as much weight and value as a soap bubble. How easy for me to give you this pledge! And all the while I may be a direct accessory in the tragedy you have resolved to unriddle."

"I thank you for reminding me," I said. "You shall swear to me that you have had no hand in this most horrible and dastardly murder."

"More inconsistency, more lack of logical perception," he said, and the magnetism in his eyes compelled me to fix my gaze upon the cross on the table. "You ask me to swear, and you will be content with my oath. I render you my obligations for your faith in my veracity. How shall I swear? How shall I deliver myself of the sacred and holy pledge? There are so many forms, so many symbols, of pledging one's mortal heart and immortal soul. The civilised Jew, when he is married to his beloved under the canopy, grinds a wine glass to dust with the heel of his boot, and the guests and relatives, especially the relatives of the bride, lift up their voices in joyful praise, with the conscious self-delusion that this sacred rite insures the faithfulness of the bridegroom to the woman he has wedded. Some burn wax candles – very bad wax often – for the release of souls from purgatory. The Chinaman, called upon for his oath, blows out a candle, twists the neck of a terrified cock, or smashes a saucer. The Christian kisses the New Testament; the Jew kisses the Old. The Christian swears with his hat off; the Jew with his hat on. I could multiply anomalies, all opposed to each other. Which kind of obligation would you prefer from me? A cock or a hen? Produce the sacred symbol, and I am ready. Shall my head be covered or uncovered? As you please. Ah, how strange! With this pencil and penholder my fingers have insensibly formed a cross. Shall I swear upon that, and will it content you? Take your choice, my dear sir, take your choice. Call me Jew, Christian, Pagan, Chinaman – which you please. I am willing to oblige you. Or shall we be sensible. Will you take my simple word for it?"

"I will," I said; "but I must have a hostage."

"Anything, anything, my dear sir. Give it a name."

"Your desk," I said, "which not unlikely contains private writings and confessions."

"It does," he replied, tapping on the desk with his knuckles. "You little dream of the treasures, the strange secrets, herein contained. You would have this as a hostage?"

"I would."

"It shall be yours, on the understanding that if I claim it from you within three months after the mystery of the murder of Lizzie Melladew is cleared up, you will deliver it to me again intact, with its contents unread."

"I promise faithfully," I said.

"I must trouble you," he said; and he suddenly placed his hand upon my forehead, and stood over me. "Yes," he said, resuming his seat, "the promise is faithfully made. You will keep it."

He locked the desk, and pushed it across the table to me, putting the key in his pocket.

"And now, your word of truth and honour," I said.

"Give me your hand. On my truth and honour I pledge myself to you. Moreover, if it will ease your mind of an absurd suspicion, I declare, on my truth and honour, that I have had nothing whatever to do with this murder."

His words carried conviction with them.

"But you will assist me in my search?" I said.

"To the extent of my power. Understand, however, that I do not undertake that your search shall be successful. It does not depend upon me; accident will probably play its part in the matter. There is a clause, moreover, in our agreement to which I require your adhesion. It is, that during your search you will do nothing to fasten publicity upon me, and that, in the event of your succeeding, I shall not be dragged into the case."

"Unless you are required as a witness," I said.

"I shall not be required. I have no evidence to offer which a court of law would accept."

"Who is to be the judge of that?"

"You yourself."

"I agree. You must not regard me as a spy upon your movements when I tell you I shall sleep in this house tonight."

"Not at all. That you are a man of mettle – a man who can form a resolution and carry it out, never mind at what inconvenience to yourself – makes your company agreeable to me. I like you; I accept you as my comrade, for a brief space, in lieu of that miserable groveller Lemon, who has no more strength of nerve than a jellyfish. Sleep in the house, and welcome. Sleep in this room."

"Where?" I asked, looking around for the accommodation.

"A shakedown on the floor. Our mutual good friend Mrs. Lemon shall bring up a mattress, a pillow, a sheet, and a pair of blankets, and you shall lie snug and warm. I do not offer you my own bed, for I know that, having the instincts of a gentleman, you would not accept it, but I offer you the hospitality of my poor apartment. We will sup together, we will sleep together, in the morning we will breakfast together, and we will go out to business together, you taking the position of poor Lemon, whom, from this moment, I cast off for ever. What say you?"

I debated with myself. It was important that I should not lose sight of Devlin; left to my own resources, I should not know how to proceed; I depended entirely upon him to supply me with a clue. But what could be his reason for proposing that we should go out to business together? Of what use could I be in a barber's shop, and how would my presence there assist me? As, however, he appeared to be dealing frankly and honestly, my best course perhaps would be to do the same. Therefore I put the questions which perplexed me in plain language.

"My dear sir," he replied, "in my place of business, and in no other place, shall we be able to find a starting-point. Do not entail upon me the necessity of saying 'upon my truth and honour' to everything I advance. Have confidence in me, and you will be a thousand pounds the richer, probably two, if the gentleman who made you the offer keeps his word."

I hesitated no longer. I would act frankly and boldly, and for the next twenty-four hours at least would be guided by him.

"I accept your hospitality," I said, "and will do as you wish."

"Good," he said, rubbing his hands; "we may regard the campaign as opened. Woe to the murderer! Justice shall overtake him; he shall hang!" He uttered these words in a tone of malignant satisfaction, and as though the prospect of any man being hanged was thoroughly agreeable to him. "I will prove to you," he continued, "how completely you can trust me. You came here today with the intention of returning home and sleeping there. Your absence will alarm your wife. You must write to her."

He placed notepaper and envelopes before me, and took from the mantelshelf a penny stone bottle of ink, then pointed to the pen which formed part of the cross upon the table.

I wrote a line to my wife, informing her that events of great importance had occurred in relation to the murder of Lizzie Melladew, and that, for the purpose of following up the threads of a possible discovery, I intended to sleep out tonight; I desired her in my letter to go and see Mr. Portland and tell him that I was engaged in the task he had intrusted to me, and believed I should soon be in possession of a clue. "Have no anxiety for me," I said; "I am quite safe, and no harm will befall me. The prospect of unravelling this dreadful mystery fills me with joy." She would know what I meant by this; the murderer discovered, we should be comparatively rich. I fastened and addressed my letter.

"It should reach her hands tonight," said Devlin. "How will you send it?"

I stepped to the window, and, looking out, distinguished the figures of George Carton and Mr. Kenneth Dowsett, Mr. Dowsett seemed to be endeavouring, unavailingly, to persuade his ward to come away with him. I could employ no better messenger than George Carton; he should take my letter to my wife. Returning to the centre of the room, my eyes fell upon Devlin's desk. Devlin smiled and nodded; he knew what was passing in my mind.

"I shall send my letter," I said, "by the hands of George Carton, who is still in the square, and I shall send your desk with it."

"Do so," said Devlin.

I opened the envelope, and tearing it into very small pieces flung them out of window. Devlin smiled again.

"So that I should not discover your address," he said.

"That is it," I replied.

"It is likely," he said, "to be not very far from Mr. Melladew, because you and he are friends."

I added a few words to my letter, desiring my wife to put the desk in a place of safety; and then, addressing another envelope, I went downstairs, bearing both desk and letter.

"I shall be here when you come back," said Devlin. "Even were I protean, I shall not change my shape. My word is given."

On my way to the street-door I encountered Fanny Lemon.

"Well, sir?" she asked anxiously.

"I will speak to you presently," I said, and, opening the street-door, crossed the road to where George Carton and his guardian were standing.

XXII

I SEND DEVLIN'S DESK TO MY WIFE, AND SMOKE A FRAGRANT CIGAR

"This foolish, headstrong lad will be the death of me," said Mr. Dowsett in a fretful tone, "and of himself as well."

"I am neither foolish nor headstrong," retorted the unhappy young man. "I told you he was in there still, and you told me he had left the house."

"I said it for your good," said Mr. Dowsett, "but you will not be ruled."

"No, I will not!" exclaimed George Carton violently; and then said remorsefully, "I beg you to forgive me for speaking so wildly; it is the height of ingratitude after all your goodness to me. But do you not see – for God's sake, do you not see – that you are making things worse instead of better for me by opposing me as you are doing? I will have my way! I will, whether I am right or wrong!"

"My poor boy," said Mr. Dowsett, addressing me, "has got it into his foolish head that you can be of some assistance to him. In heaven's name, how can you be?"

"Mr. Dowsett," I said, and the strange experiences of the last few hours imported, I felt, a solemnity into my voice, "the ends of justice are sometimes reached by roads we cannot see. It may be so in this sad instance."

"There," said George Carton to his guardian, in a tone of melancholy triumph, "did I not tell you?"

Mr. Dowsett shrugged his shoulders impatiently, and said, "I declare that if I did not love my ward with a love as sincere and perfect as any human being ever felt for another, I would wash my hands of this business altogether."

"But why," said Carton, with much affection, "do you torment yourself about it at all?"

"It is you I torment myself about," said Mr. Dowsett, "not the horrible deed. I love you with a father's love, and I cannot leave you in the state you are."

George Carton put his arm around his guardian caressingly. "I am not worth it," he murmured; "I am not worth it; but I cannot act otherwise than I do. Sir" – to me – "I have lingered here in the hope that you might have some news to tell me."

"I have nothing I can communicate to you," I said; "but rest assured that my interest in the discovery of the murderer is scarcely less than yours. I have taken up the search, and I will not rest while there is the shadow of a hope left."

"I knew it, I knew it," said George Carton.

"Knowing it, then," I said, "and receiving the assurance from my lips, will you do me a service, and be guided by my advice?"

"I will, indeed I will," replied Carton.

"It is heartbreaking," said Mr. Dowsett mournfully, turning his head, "to find a stranger's counsel preferred to mine."

"No, no," cried George Carton, "I declare to you, no! But you would have me do nothing, and I cannot obey you. I cannot – I cannot sit idly down, and make no effort in the cause of justice. My dear Lizzie is dead, and I do not care to live. But I will live for one thing – revenge!"

"Be calm," I said, taking the young man's fevered hand, "and listen to me. I wish you to take this letter and desk to my wife, and deliver them to her with your own hands. Will you do so?"

"Yes."

"You must not part with them under any pretext or persuasion until you place them in my wife's possession."

"No one shall touch them till she receives them."

"You must go at once, for she is anxious about me. I intend to sleep here tonight. And when you have done what I ask you, I beg you to go home with your guardian, and have a good night's rest."

He looked discontented at this, but Mr. Dowsett said, "Be persuaded, George, be persuaded!"

"Believe me," I said, speaking very earnestly, "that it will be for the best."

"Very well, sir. I will do as you desire. But" – turning to Mr. Dowsett – "no opiates. If sleep comes to me, it shall come naturally."

"I promise you, George," said Mr. Dowsett; "and now let us go. Thank you, sir, thank you a thousand times, for having prevailed upon my ward to do what is right. Come, George, come."

He was so anxious to get the young man away that he advanced a few steps quickly; thus for two or three moments Carton and I were alone.

"Shall I see you tomorrow, sir," asked Carton.

"In all probability," I replied; "but do not seek me here. I have your address, and will either call upon or write to you."

"Then I am to remain home all day?"

"Yes. By following my instructions you will be rendering me practical assistance."

"Very well, sir. I put all my trust in you."

"Are you coming, George?" cried Mr. Dowsett, looking back.

"Yes, I am ready," said the young man, joining his guardian; and presently they were both out of sight.

I reëntered the house. Fanny Lemon was still in the passage.

"Fanny," I said, "I cannot keep long with you, as I have business upstairs with Mr. Devlin; but I wish to impress upon you not to speak to a single soul of what has passed between us today. Say nothing to anybody about Mr. Lemon being ill, and, above all, do not call in a doctor. Doctors are apt to be inquisitive, and it is of the highest importance that curiosity shall not be aroused in the minds of the neighbours. There is nothing radically wrong with Lemon; he has received a fright, and his nerves are shaken, that is all. Tell him that I have taken his place with Devlin, and that the partnership is at an end. That will relieve his mind. Keep him quiet, and give him nothing to drink but milk or barley water. Lower his system, Fanny, lower his system."

"Don't you think it low enough already, sir?" asked Fanny.

"I do not; he is in a state of dangerous excitement, and everything must be done to soothe and quiet him. But I have no more time to waste. You will do as I have told you?"

"Yes, sir, I'll be careful to. But are you sure he don't want a doctor? Are you sure he won't die?"

"Quite sure; and you can tell him, if you like, that *I* say it is all right."

"*Is* it all right, sir?"

"If it isn't, I'm going to try to make it so. I shall sleep here tonight, Fanny."

"And welcome, sir. We haven't a spare bedroom, but I can make you up a bed on the sofa in the parlour."

"I shall not need it. I am going to sleep in Devlin's room, on the floor."

She caught my arm with a cry of alarm. "Has he got hold of you, too, sir? The Lord save us! He's got the lot of us in his claws!"

"Don't be absurd," I said. "I know what I'm about, and Mr. Devlin will find me a match for him. No more questions; do as you are bid. If you have a mattress and some bedclothes to spare, bring them up at once."

"I won't look at him, sir – I won't speak to him! O, how shall I ever forgive myself – how shall I ever forgive myself?"

She threw her apron (which during my absence she had put on over her faded black silk dress) over her head, and swayed to and fro in the passage, moaning and groaning in great distress of mind.

I pulled the apron from her face, and gave her a good shaking by way of corrective. She ceased her moans.

"I have no patience with you, Fanny," I exclaimed. "In heaven's name, what do you want to be forgiven for?"

"For dragging you into this horrible business, sir," she said, with a tendency to relapse, which I immediately checked by another shaking. "That – that devil upstairs—"

This time I shook her so soundly that she could not get out another word for the chattering of her teeth.

"No more, Fanny," I said roughly, "or you will make me angry. I know what I am about, and if you don't stop instantly and do exactly as I bid you, I'll leave you and your Lemon to your fate. Do you hear?"

The threat terrified her into calmness.

"I'll bring up the bed-things, sir," she said, with bated breath.

"And lose no time," I said, as I mounted the stairs.

"I won't, sir."

Devlin was smoking when I joined him, and not smoking a pipe, but a cigar with a most delicious fragrance.

"Take one," he said, pushing a cigar-case over to me; "you will find them good. I manufactured them while you were away."

I bore good-humouredly with his banter, and I took a cigar from the case, but did not immediately light it.

"Sent your letter?" he inquired curtly.

"Yes."

"And my desk?"

"Yes."

"By Lizzie Melladew's sweetheart?"

"Yes."

"Not by the other?"

"No."

"Do they live together?"

"Yes."

"Do you know where?"

"Yes."

"Capital!" he said, with the air of a man who had been asking important instead of trivial questions. "There is a knock at the door – a frightened, feminine knock. Enter, my dear Mrs. Lemon, enter."

Fanny Lemon came in, smothered with a mattress, sheets, blankets, and pillows, and, without uttering a word, proceeded to make the bed on the floor.

"You have brought plenty of pillows, Fanny," I remarked.

"I thought you'd like to lay high, sir," she whispered.

Devlin broke out into a loud laugh. "Most people do," he said, "while they live. When they die they all lie low—all of them, all of them!"

For a moment I thought that Fanny was going to run away, but a look from me restrained her, and she finished making the bed.

"Do you wish anything else, sir?" she asked, still in a whisper, and keeping her back to Devlin.

"Yes, my charming landlady, yes," replied Devlin, "A large pot of your exquisite tea. Fly!"

"Make it, Fanny, and bring it up," I said.

She flew, and returned with the steaming pot. Surely never was tea so quickly prepared before. The pot, milk, sugar, and two cups and saucers were on a tray, which, without raising her eyes, she placed before me.

"Here, here," cried Devlin, tapping the table. "Before *me*, my dear creature! *I* am the host on this occasion."

She slid the tray over to him, and he made a motion as if he were about to place his hand on her.

"If you lay a finger on me," she exclaimed, beating a hasty retreat from the table, "I'll scream the house down!"

"Leave the room," I said sternly; "and call us at seven in the morning."

"We shall be here, my dear creature," added Devlin. "You will find both of us safe and sound, ready to do justice to your excellent cooking. I have a premonition of a fine appetite for breakfast; cook me an extra rasher."

I saw in Fanny's eyes a desire to say a word to me alone. Devlin saw it too.

"Humour her," he said, and quoted a line from a comedy. "What is the use of a friend if you can't make a stranger of him?"

I followed Fanny into the passage.

"You've quite made up your mind, sir?"

"Quite, Fanny."

"Take this, sir," she said, pushing a hard substance into my hands. "If anything happens in the night, spring it."

It was a policeman's rattle.

"I don't know where Lemon got it from," she said, "but we've had it in the house for years."

"Pshaw, Fanny!" I said, forcing the rattle back into her hands. "You are too ridiculous!"

Yet when I was once again face to face with Devlin, with the door locked, I could not help thinking that I was acting a perilous part in putting myself, as it were, into his power. He might kill me while I slept. I determined to keep awake, and to lie down in my clothes.

"Have some tea?" he asked.

"Thank you," I replied. The tea would assist me in my resolve not to sleep.

The teapot being emptied, I lit the cigar Devlin had given me.

"I owe you an explanation," he said, puffing the smoke from his cigar into a series of circles. "I take it as a fact that Lemon is suffering from some kind of prophetic vision in connection with the murder of Lizzie Melladew in Victoria Park on Friday night."

"It is so," I said.

"Part of my explanation lies in the admission that he received that forewarning from me."

"Then you knew it was done," I cried.

"I did not know it. It passed through the mind of a customer whose hair I was dressing. I do not call that knowing a thing. I am something of a thought-reader, my dear sir, and I possess a certain power, under suitable conditions, of conveying my impressions to another person. That is the extent of my explanation. Excuse me for making it so brief."

Never in my life had I smoked a cigar with a fragrance so exquisite. Not only exquisite, but overpowering. It beguiled my senses, and had such an effect upon me that the last twenty or thirty words uttered by Devlin seemed to be spoken at a great distance from me. This sense of distance affected not only his voice, but himself and all surrounding things. He and they seemed to recede into space, as it were, not bounded by the walls of the small apartment in which we were sitting. I had a dim desire to continue the conversation, and to press Devlin to be more explicit, but it died away. Everything floated in a mist around me, and in this state I fell asleep.

XXIII

I PASS A MORNING IN DEVLIN'S PLACE OF BUSINESS

Devlin was up and dressed when I awoke in the morning. I had not to go through the trouble of putting on my clothes, as I had not taken them off on the previous night. It would not have surprised me to find that I had unconsciously sought repose in the usual way, or that I had risen in my sleep to undress; nothing, indeed, would very much have surprised me, so strange had been my dreaming fancies. Naturally they all turned upon Devlin and the case upon which I was engaged. I could easily write a chapter upon them, but I will content myself with briefly describing one of the strangest of them all.

I was sitting in a chair, opposite a mirror, in which I saw everything that was passing in the room. Devlin was standing over me, dressing my hair. Suddenly I saw a sharp surgical instrument in his hand.

"That is not a razor," I said, "and I don't want to be shaved."

"My dear sir," remarked Devlin, with excessive politeness, "what you want or what you don't want matters little."

With that he made a straight cut across the top of my head, and laid bare my brains. I saw them and every little cell in them quite distinctly.

"To think," he observed, as he peered into the cavities, "that in this small compass should abide the passions, the emotions, the meannesses, the noble aspirations, the sordid desires, the selfish instincts and the power to resist them, the sense of duty, the conscious deceits, the lust for power, the grovelling worship, the filthy qualities of animalism, the secret promptings, and all the motley mental and moral attributes which make a man! To think that from this small compass have sprung all that constitutes man's history – religion, ethics, the rise and fall of nations, music, poetry, law, and science! How grand, how noble does this man, who represents humankind, think himself! What works he has executed, what marvels discovered! But if the truth were known, he is a mere dabbler, who, out of his conceit, magnifies the smallest of molehills into the largest of mountains. He can build a bridge, but he cannot make a flower that shall bloom today and die tomorrow. He can destroy, but he cannot create. In the open page of Nature he makes the most trivial of discoveries, and he straightway writes himself up in letters of gold and builds monuments in his honour. The stars mock him; the mountains of snow look loftily down upon the pigmy; the gossamer fly which his eyes can scarcely see triumphs over his highest efforts. But he has invented for himself a supreme shelter for defeat and decay. Dear me, dear me – I cannot find it!"

"What are you looking for?" I asked. "Be kind enough to leave my brains alone." For he was industriously probing them with some sensitive instrument.

"I am looking for your grand invention, your soul. I am wondrously wise, but I have never yet been able to discover its precise locality."

After some further search he shut up my head, so to speak, and my fancies took another direction.

All these vagaries seemed to be tumbling over each other in my brain as I rose from my bed on the floor.

"Had a good night?" asked Devlin.

"If being asleep," I replied, "means having a good night, I have had it. But my head is in a whirl, nevertheless."

"Keep it cool if you can," said Devlin, "for what you have to go through. You will find water and soap inside."

He pointed to the little closet adjoining his room, and there I found all that was necessary for my toilet. I had just finished when Fanny knocked at the door.

"It's all right, Fanny," I cried. "You can get breakfast ready."

"And don't forget," added Devlin, "the extra rasher for me. How is dear Lemon?"

That she did not reply and was heard beating a hasty retreat caused a broad grin to spread over Devlin's face.

"I have provided," he said, "for that worthy creature something of an entertaining, not to say enthralling, nature, which she can dilate upon to the last hour of her life. And yet she is not grateful."

We went down to breakfast, and there I was afforded an opportunity of verifying the subtle likeness in Devlin's face to the portrait of Lemon on the wall, the evil-looking bird in its glass case, and the stone figure, half monster, half man, on the mantel-shelf.

"There is a likeness," said Devlin pleasantly, "between my works and me, and if you will attribute me with anything human, you can attribute it to a common human failing. It springs from the vanity and the weakness of man that he can evolve only that which is within himself. Nowhere is that vanity and weakness more conspicuous than in Genesis, in the very first chapter, my dear sir, where man himself has had the audacity to write that 'God created man in His own image.' My dear Mrs. Lemon, you have excelled yourself this morning. This rasher is perfect, and your cooking of these eggs to the infinitesimal part of a second is a marvel of art."

Fanny did not open her lips to him, and the meal passed on in silence so far as she was concerned. I made a good breakfast, and Devlin expressed approval of my appetite.

"It will strengthen you," he said, "for what is before you."

Fanny looked up in alarm, and Devlin laughed. I may mention that the first thing I did when I came downstairs was to run to the nearest newspaper shop and purchase copies of the morning papers.

"Is there anything new concerning the murder?" asked Devlin.

Fanny waited breathlessly for my reply.

"Nothing," I said.

"Have any arrests been made?"

"None."

"Of course," observed Devlin sarcastically, "the police are on the track of the murderer."

"There is something to that effect in the papers."

"Fudge!" said Devlin.

Breakfast over, Devlin said he would go up to his room for a few minutes, and bade me be ready when he came down. Alone with Fanny, she asked me whether I would like to see Lemon, adding that it would do him "a power of good."

"Is he any better?" I asked.

"I really think he is," she replied. "What I told him last night about your taking up the case was a comfort to him – though he ain't easy in his mind about you. He is afraid that Devlin will get hold of you as he did of him."

"He will not, Fanny. We shall get along famously together."

She shook her head. I failed to convince her, as I failed to convince Mr. Lemon, that I should prove a match for their lodger. Lemon presented a ludicrous picture, sitting up in bed with an old-fashioned nightcap on.

"Don't go with him, sir," he whispered, "to the Twisted Cow."

"I shall go with him," I said, "wherever he proposes to take me."

I could not help smiling at Lemon's expression of melancholy as I made this statement. He dared not give utterance to his fears of what my ultimate destination would be if I continued to keep company with Devlin. When that strange personage came down I was ready for him, and we went out together, Fanny looking after us from the street-door, shaking, I well knew, in her inward soul.

Devlin made himself exceedingly pleasant, and the comments he passed on the people we met excited my admiration and increased my wonder. He seemed to be able to read their characters in their faces, and although I would have liked to combat his views I did not venture to oppose my judgment to his. What struck me particularly was that he saw the evil in men, not the good. Not once did he give man or woman credit for the possession of good qualities. All was mean, sordid, grasping, and selfish. He told me that we should have to walk four miles to his place of business.

"I enjoy walking," he said, "and the only riding I care for is on the top of an omnibus through squalid streets. You get peeps into garrets and one-room habitations. Gifted with the power of observation, you can see rare pictures there."

On our road I stopped at a post-office, and sent a telegram of three words to my wife: "All is well."

Our course lay in the direction of Westminster. We crossed the bridge, and turned down a narrow street. Chapel Street. Halfway down the street Devlin paused, and said,

"Behold our establishment."

It was a poor and common house, and had it not been for a barber's pole sticking out from the doorway, and a fly-blown cardboard in the parlour window, on which was written, "Barber and Hairdresser. All styles. Lowest charges," I should not have supposed that a trade was carried on therein. As we entered the passage a woman came forward and handed Devlin a key. He thanked her, unlocked the parlour door, and we went in.

The fittings in this room, which I saw at a glance was the shop in which the shaving and hair-dressing were done, were entirely out of keeping with the poor tenement in which it was situated. The walls were lined with fine mirrors; there were three luxurious barber's chairs; the washstands were of marble; and the appliances for shampooing perfect.

"You would hardly expect it," observed Devlin.

"I would not," I replied.

"It is my idea," he said. "It rivals the West End establishments, and for skill I would challenge the world, if I were desirous of courting publicity. Then, the charges. One-sixth those of Truefit. I shave for a penny, cut for another penny, shampoo for another. But only those can be attended to who hold my tickets. I was compelled to adopt this plan, otherwise I should have been overwhelmed with customers. It enables me to choose them. When I see a likely man, one who is ripe, and in whom I discern possibilities which commend themselves to me, I say, 'Oblige me, sir, by accepting this ticket of admission;' and having given him a taste of my skill, he comes again. I have quite a connection." He accompanied these last words with a strange smile.

"What part do you propose to assign to me in the business?" I asked.

"A part to which you will not object, that of looker-on. Not from this room, but that" – pointing to the back room. "The panels of the door, you will observe, are of ground glass. Sitting within there, you can see all that passes in this room without being yourself seen. If you will keep quiet, no one will suspect that you are in hiding."

"For the life of me," I said, "I cannot guess what good my sitting in there will do."

"I do not suppose you can; but learn from me that I do nothing without a motive. I do not care to be questioned too closely. The promise I have made to you will be kept if you do not thwart it. You may see something that will surprise you. I say 'may,' because I have not the power to entirely rule men's movements. But I think it almost certain he will pay me a visit this morning."

"He?" I cried. "Who?"

"The man whose thoughts I read on Friday with respect to the girl who was murdered on that night."

I started. If Devlin spoke the truth, and if the man came to his shop this morning, I should be in possession of a practical clue which would lead me to the goal I wished to reach.

"He comes regularly," continued Devlin, "on Mondays, Wednesdays, and Fridays. This is his day."

"Do you know his name?" I inquired, in great excitement.

"I did not," replied Devlin, "the last time I saw him. How should I know it now?"

"Nor where he lives?"

"Nor where he lives."

"I must obey you, I suppose," I said.

"It will be advisable, and you must obey me implicitly. Deviate by a hair's breadth from what I require of you, and I withdraw my promise, which now exists in full integrity. Decide."

"I have decided. I will remain in that room."

"There is another point upon which I must insist positively. From that room you do not stir until I bid you; in that room you do not speak unless you receive a cue from me. Agreed?"

"Agreed."

"On your honour?"

"On my honour."

"Good. Now you can retire. You will find books in there to amuse you if you get wearied with your watch."

He opened the door for me, and closed it upon me. He had spoken correctly. Through the ground glass I could see everything in the shop, and I took his word for it that I could not myself be seen.

Scarcely had a minute passed before a customer entered. Devlin, who, while he was arguing with me, had taken off his coat, and put on a linen jacket of spotless white, behaved most decorously. His manner was deferential without being subservient, respectful without being familiar. The man was shaved by Devlin, and then his head was brushed by machinery, which I had forgotten to mention was fixed in the shop. There was a caressing motion about Devlin's shapely hands which could not but be agreeable to those who sought his tonsorial aid, and his conversation, judging from the expression on his customer's face, must have been amusing and entertaining. The customer took his departure, and another, appearing as he went out, was duly attended to. This went on until eleven o'clock by my watch, and nothing had occurred of especial interest to me. Devlin was kept pretty busy; but, although his time was fully employed, the business at such prices could not have been remunerative, especially when it was considered that the fitting up of the shop must have cost a pretty sum of money, and that the profits of the concern had to be divided between two persons, Mr. Lemon and himself. It was not till past eleven that my attention was more than ordinarily attracted by Devlin's behaviour, the difference in which perhaps no one except myself would have particularly noticed. A man of the middle class entered and took his seat. He wore a beard and moustache; and although I could not hear what he said, he spoke in so low a tone, I judged correctly that he instructed Devlin to shave his face bare. Devlin proceeded to obey him, and clipped and cut, and finally applied his razor until not a vestige of hair was left on the man's face. That being done, Devlin cut this customer's hair close, and then used his brushes; and as his hands moved about the man's head there was, if I may so describe it, a feline, insinuating expression in them which aroused my curiosity.

I thought of the singular dream I have described, and it appeared to me that all the while Devlin was employed over his customer the brains of the man sitting so quietly in the chair were figuratively exposed to his view, and that he was reading the thoughts which stirred therein. When the man was gone there was a peculiar smile upon Devlin's face, and I observed that he laughed quietly to himself. There happened to be no one in the shop to claim Devlin's attention, and I, who was impatiently waiting for some sign from Devlin pertinent to the secret purpose to which both he and I were pledged, expected it to be given now; for the circumstance of the man having been shaved bare – which so altered his appearance that I should not otherwise have known that the person who entered the shop was the same person who left it – was to me so suspicious that in my anxiety and agitation I connected it with the murder of poor Lizzie Melladew, arguing that the man had effected this disguise in himself for the purpose of escaping detection. But Devlin made no sign, and did not even look towards the glass-door. Other customers coming in, Devlin was busy again. Twelve o'clock – half-past twelve – one o'clock – and still no indication of anything in connection with my task. With a feeling of intense disappointment, and beginning to doubt whether I had not allowed myself to be duped, I replaced my watch in my pocket, and had scarcely done so before my heart was beating violently at the appearance of a gentleman whom I little expected to see in Devlin's shop. This gentleman was no other than Mr. Kenneth Dowsett, George Carton's guardian.

XXIV

MR. KENNETH DOWSETT GIVES ME THE SLIP

The beating of my heart became normal; I suppose it was the sudden appearance of a gentleman with whose face I was familiar, after many hours of suspense, that had caused its pulsations to become so rapid and violent. There was nothing surprising, after all, in the presence of Mr. Dowsett in Devlin's shop. His address was in Westminster, Devlin was an exceptionally fine workman, the accommodation was luxurious, the charges low. Even I, in my position in life, would be tempted to deal occasionally with so expert and perfect a barber as Devlin, at the prices he charged. Then, why not Mr. Kenneth Dowsett? Besides, he might be of a frugal turn.

Devlin was not long engaged over him. Mr. Dowsett was shaved; Mr. Dowsett had his hair brushed by machinery; Mr. Dowsett, moreover, was very particular as to the arrangement of his hair; and Devlin, I saw, did his best to please him. But so deft and facile was Devlin that he did not dally with Mr. Dowsett for longer than five or six minutes. Mr. Dowsett rose, paid Devlin, exchanged a few smiling words with him, and taking a final look at himself in the mirrors, turning himself this way and that, walked out of the shop. Evidently Mr. Dowsett was a very vain man.

No sooner was he gone than Devlin locked the shop-door from within, whipped off his linen jacket, and opened the door of the room in which I was sitting. I came forward in no amiable mood.

"You are wearied with your long enforced rest," said Devlin.

"I am wearied and disgusted," I retorted. "I expected a clue."

"Have you not received it?" asked Devlin, smiling.

"Received it!" I echoed. "How? Where?"

"You have seen my customers, and all that has passed between me and them."

"Well?"

"Well?" he said, mocking me. "Is there not one among them upon whom your suspicions are fixed? Is there not one among them who could, if he chose, supply us with a starting-point? I say 'us,' because we are comrades."

"Fool, fool, that I was!" I exclaimed, involuntarily raising my hand to my forehead. "Why did I allow him to escape?"

"Why did you let whom escape you?" asked Devlin, in a bantering tone.

"The man whose beard and moustache you shaved off. He must have a reason, a vital reason, for effecting this disguise in himself. And I have let him slip through my fingers!"

"He has a vital reason for so disguising himself," said Devlin, "but it has no connection with the murder of Lizzie Melladew."

"Then what do you mean?" I cried, "by asking me whether I have not received a clue?"

"Was your attention attracted to no other of my customers than this man?"

"There was only one who was known to me – Mr. Kenneth Dowsett."

"Ah!" said Devlin. "Mr. Kenneth Dowsett."

A light seemed to dawn suddenly upon me, but the suggestion conveyed in Devlin's significant tone so amazed me that I could not receive it unquestioningly.

"Do you mean to tell me," I cried, "that you suspect Mr. Dowsett of complicity in this frightful murder?"

"I mean to tell you nothing of my suspicions," replied Devlin. "It is for you, not for me, to suspect. It is for you, not for me, to draw conclusions. What I know positively of Mr. Dowsett – with whose name I was unacquainted until last evening, when you mentioned it in Lemon's house – I will tell you, if you wish."

"Tell me, then."

"It is short but pregnant. Through Mr. Kenneth Dowsett's mind, as I shaved him and dressed his hair on Friday last, passed the picture of a beautiful girl, with golden hair, wearing a bunch of white daisies in her belt. Through his mind passed a picture of a lake of still water in Victoria Park. Through his mind passed a vision of blood."

"Are you a devil," I exclaimed, "that you did not step in to prevent the deed?"

"My dear sir," he said, seizing my arm, which I had involuntarily raised, and holding it as in a vice, "you are unreasonable. I have never in my life been in Victoria Park, which, I believe, covers a large space of ground. Why should I elect to pass an intensely uncomfortable night, wandering about paths in an unknown place, to interfere in I know not what? Even were I an interested party, it would be an act of folly, for such a proceeding would lay me open to suspicion. A nice task you would allot to me when you tacitly declare that it should be my mission to prevent the commission of human crime! Then how was I to gauge the precise value of Mr. Dowsett's thoughts? He might be a dramatist, inventing a sensational plot for a popular theatre; he might be an author of exciting fiction. Give over your absurdities, and school yourself into calmer methods. Unless you do so, you will have small chance of unravelling this mystery. And consider, my dear sir," he added, making me a mocking bow, "if I am a devil, how honoured you should be that I accept you as my comrade!"

The tone in which he spoke was calm and measured; indeed, it had not escaped my observation that, whether he was inclined to be malignant or agreeable, insinuating or threatening, he never raised his voice above a certain pitch. I inwardly acknowledged the wisdom of his counsel that I should keep my passion in control, and I resolved from that moment to follow it.

"You locked the shop-door," I said, "when Mr. Dowsett left you just now."

"I did," was his response, "thinking it would be your wish that I should do no more business today."

"Why should you think that?"

"Because of what was passing through Mr. Dowsett's mind."

"I ask you to pardon me for my display of passion. What was Mr. Dowsett thinking of?"

"Of two very simple matters," said Devlin; "the time of day and an address. The time was fifteen minutes past three, the address, 28 Athelstan Road."

"Nothing more?" I inquired, much puzzled.

"Nothing more."

I pondered a moment; I could draw no immediate conclusion from material so bare. I asked Devlin what he could make of it; he replied, politely, that it was for me, not for him, to make what I could of it. A suggestion presented itself.

"At fifteen minutes past three," I said, "Mr. Dowsett has an appointment with some person at 28 Athelstan Road."

"Possibly," said Devlin.

"Have you a 'London Directory'?"

"I have not; nor, I imagine, will you easily find one in this neighbourhood."

"A simpler plan," I said, "perhaps will be to go to Mr. Dowsett's house, to which he has most likely returned, and set watch there for him, keeping ourselves well out of sight. It is now twenty minutes past one; we can reach his house in ten minutes. He will hardly leave it for his appointment till two, or a little past. We will follow him secretly, and ascertain whom he is going to see, and his purpose. I am determined now to adopt bold measures. Behind this frightful mystery there is another, which shall be brought to light. You will accompany me?"

"I am at your orders," said Devlin.

We left the house together, and in the time I specified were within a few yards of Mr. Dowsett's residence. Aware of the importance of not attracting attention, I looked about for a means of escaping observation. Nearly opposite Mr. Dowsett's dwelling was a public-house, in the first-floor window of which I saw a placard, "Billiards. Pool." I concluded that it was the window of a billiard-room, and without hesitation I entered the public-house, followed by Devlin, and mounted the stairs. The room, as I supposed, contained a billiard-table; the marker, a very pale and very thin youth, was practising the spot stroke.

"Billiards, sir?" he asked, as we entered.

"Yes," I said, "we wish to play a private game. How much an hour?"

"Eighteenpence."

"Here are five shillings," I said, "for a couple of hours. We shall not want you to mark. Don't let us be disturbed."

The pale thin youth took the money, laid down his cue, and left us to ourselves. When he was gone I placed a chair at an angle against the handle of the door, there being no key in the lock, and thus prevented the entrance of any person without notice. It was the leisure time of the day, and there was little fear of our being disturbed. The extra gratuity I had given to the marker would insure privacy. As I took my station at the window, from which Mr. Dowsett's house was in full view, Devlin nodded approval of my proceedings.

"You are a man of resource," he said. "I perceive that you intend henceforth to act sensibly."

Minute after minute passed, and there was no sign of any person leaving or entering Mr. Dowsett's house. Every now and then I consulted my watch. Two o'clock – a quarter-past two – half-past. I began to grow impatient, but, to please Devlin, did not exhibit it. Perfect silence reigned between us; we exchanged not a word.

Time waned, and now I more frequently looked at my watch, the hands of which were drawing on to three. They reached the hour and passed it. A quarter-past three.

Perplexed and disappointed, I debated on my next move. I soon decided what it should be. I had promised Richard Carton that I would call upon him. I would do so now. If Mr. Dowsett was at home, all the better.

I made Devlin acquainted with my resolve, and he said,

"Very good; I will go with you."

Removing the chair I had placed against the handle of the door, we went from the public-house and crossed the road. I knocked at Mr. Dowsett's door, and a maidservant answered the summons.

"Does Mr. Kenneth Dowsett live here?"

"Yes, sir."

"Is he at home?"

"No, sir."

"Is Mr. Richard Carton in?"

"Yes, sir."

"Give him my card, and say I wish to see him."

"Will you please walk this way, sir?" said the maidservant.

She ushered us into the dining-room, where she left us alone while she went to apprise Richard Carton of my visit. The room was exceedingly well furnished. Good pictures were on the walls, and there was a tasteful arrangement of bric-a-brac and bronzes. I had no time for further observation, the entrance of Richard Carton claiming my attention.

"Ah!" he exclaimed, "you have come. I was beginning to be afraid you would disappoint me."

"You delivered my letter to my wife?" I asked.

"Yes, and the desk. My guardian wanted to persuade me to leave it till this morning, but I would not."

"You were quite right."

He looked towards Devlin.

"A friend," I said, waving my hand as a kind of introduction, "who may be of assistance to us."

"But introduce us plainly," expostulated Devlin.

"Mr. Devlin," I said, "Mr. Richard Carton."

They shook hands, and then Carton inquired whether I had anything to tell him.

"Nothing tangible," I replied, "but we are on the road."

"Yes," repeated Devlin, "we are on the road."

"Excuse me for asking," said Carton to Devlin, "but are you a detective?"

"In a spiritual way," said Devlin.

Carton's mind was too deeply occupied with the one supreme subject of the murder to ask for an explanation of this enigmatical reply. He turned towards me.

"Is your guardian in?" I inquired.

"No," said Carton.

What should I say next? It would have been folly to make Richard Carton a participant in the strange revelations which were directing my proceedings.

"Can you tell me," I asked, "where Athelstan Road is?"

"It is in Margate," he replied, in a tone of surprise, "and the number is 28."

It was my turn now to exhibit surprise. "No. 28!" I exclaimed. "Who lives there?"

"I don't know. Mrs. Dowsett and Letitia went to Margate by an early train on Saturday morning, before I was awake, and my guardian has gone there to see them. I should have proposed to go with him had it not been for my determination not to leave London till this dreadful mystery was cleared up; and then there was the promise you made me give you last night, that I should remain here all the day till you came to see me."

"When did your guardian go to Margate?" I asked.

"He has gone from Victoria," replied Carton, glancing at a marble clock on the mantelshelf, "by the Granville train. It starts at fifteen minutes past three."

I also glanced at the clock. It was just half-past three, a quarter of an hour past the time!

XXV

WE FOLLOW IN PURSUIT

Carton, noticing my discomposure, inquired if there was anything wrong. I answered, yes; I was afraid there was something very wrong.

"In connection with the fate of my poor girl?" he asked.

"Yes," I replied, "in connection with her fate."

"Great heavens!" he cried. "You surely do not suspect that my guardian is mixed up with it?"

"I am of the opinion," I answered guardedly, "that he may be able to throw some light on it. Mr. Carton, ask me no further questions, or you may seriously hamper me. Have you a timetable in the house? No? Then we must obtain one immediately. It is my purpose to follow your guardian to Margate by the quickest and earliest train. I give you five minutes to get ready."

Greatly excited, he darted from the room, and in half the time I had named returned, with a small bag, into which he had thrust a few articles of clothing. During his absence I said to Devlin,

"You will accompany us?"

"My dear sir," he replied, "I will go with you to the ends of the earth. I shall greatly enjoy this pursuit; the vigour and spirit you are putting into it are worthy of the highest admiration."

We three went out together, and at the first bookshop I purchased an "A B C," and ascertained that the next best train to Margate was the 5.15 from Victoria, which was timed to arrive at 7.31. Calculating that it would be a few minutes late, we could, no doubt, reach Athelstan Road at half-past eight. I had time to run home to my wife, and embrace her and my children; it was necessary, also, that I should furnish myself with funds, there being very little money in my purse, and I determined to use the one hundred pounds which Mr. Portland had left with me. Employed as I was, the use of this money was justifiable. Hailing a hansom, we jumped into it. Carton sitting on Devlin's knee, and we soon reached my house. In as few words as possible I explained to my wife all that was necessary, kissed her and the children, took possession of the hundred pounds and of a light bag in which my wife had put a change of clothing, left a private message for Mr. Portland, and rejoined Devlin and Carton, who were waiting for me in the hansom. I asked my wife but two questions – the first, how Mr. and Mrs. Melladew were, the second, whether anything had been heard of the missing daughter Mary. She told me that the unhappy parents were completely prostrated by the blow, and that no news whatever had been heard of Mary.

We arrived at Victoria Station in good time, and, by the aid of a judicious tip, I secured a first-class compartment, into which the guard assured me no one should be admitted. I had a distinct reason for desiring this privacy. There were subjects upon which I wished to talk with Richard Carton, and I could not carry on the conversation in the presence of strangers. I said nothing to him of this in the cab, the noise of the wheels making conversation difficult. We should be two hours and a half getting to Margate, and on the journey I could obtain all the information I desired. We started promptly to the minute, and then I requested Carton to give me his best attention. He and I sat next to each other, Devlin sitting in the opposite corner. He threw himself back, and closed his eyes, but I knew that he heard every word that passed between me and Carton.

"I am going to ask you a series of questions," I said to the young man, "not one of which shall be asked from idle curiosity. Answer me as directly to the point as you can. Explain how it is that Mr. Kenneth Dowsett is your guardian."

"I lost both my parents," replied Carton, "when I was very young. Of my mother I have no remembrance whatever; of my father, but little. He and Mr. Dowsett were upon the most intimate terms of friendship; my father had such confidence in him that when he drew his will he named Mr. Dowsett as his executor and my guardian. I was to live with him and his wife, and he was to see to my education. He has faithfully fulfilled the trust my father reposed in him."

"Did your father leave a large fortune?"

"Roughly speaking, I am worth two thousand pounds a year."

"Mr. Dowsett, having to receive you in his house as a son and to look after your education, doubtless was in receipt of a fair consideration for his services?"

"O, yes. Until I was twenty-one years of age he was to draw six hundred pounds a year out of the funds invested for me. The balance accumulated for my benefit until I came of age."

"He drew this money regularly?"

"Yes, as he was entitled to do."

"How old are you now?"

"Twenty-four."

"You are living still with Mr. Dowsett, and you still regard him as your guardian?"

"I have a great affection for him; he has treated me most kindly."

"What do you pay him for your board and lodging?"

"He continues to receive the six hundred a year. It is all he has to depend on."

"Was this last arrangement of his own proposing, or yours?"

"Of mine. I cannot sufficiently repay him for his care of me."

"In your father's will what was to become of your fortune in the event of your death?"

"If I died before I came of age, my guardian was to have the six hundred a year, and the rest was to be given to various charities."

"And after you came of age?"

"It was mine absolutely, to do as I pleased with."

"Have you made a will?"

"Yes."

"Who proposed that?"

"My guardian."

"What are the terms of this will?"

"I have left everything to him. I have no relatives, and no other claims upon me."

"When I came to see you this afternoon you mentioned a name which was new to me. You said that your guardian had gone to Margate with his wife and 'Letitia.' I supposed he was married, and your speaking of Mrs. Dowsett did not surprise me. But who is Letitia?"

"Their daughter."

"An only child?"

"Yes."

"What is her age?"

"Twenty-two."

"Has she a sweetheart? Is she engaged to be married?"

"No."

"That answer seems to me to be given with constraint."

"Well," said Carton, "it is hardly right, is it, to go so minutely into my guardian's private family affairs?"

"It is entirely right. I am engaged upon a very solemn task, and I can see, probably, what is hidden from you. Why were you partly disinclined to answer my last question?"

"It is a little awkward," replied Carton, "because, perhaps, I am not quite free from blame."

"Explain your meaning. Believe me, this may be more serious than you imagine. Speak frankly. I am acting, indeed, as your true friend."

"Yet, after all," said Carton, with hesitation, "I never made love to her, I give you my honour."

"Made love to whom? Miss Dowsett?"

"Yes. The fact is they looked upon it as a settled thing that I was to marry Letitia. I did not know it at the time; no, though we were living in the same house for so many years, I never suspected it. I always looked upon Letitia as a sister, and I behaved affectionately towards her. They must have put a wrong construction upon it. When they discovered that I was in love with my poor Lizzie, Mr. Dowsett said to me, 'It will break Letitia's heart.' Then I began to understand, and I assure you I felt remorseful. Letitia did not say anything to me, but I could see by her looks how deeply she was wounded. Once my guardian made the remark, 'That if I had not met the young lady' – meaning Lizzie – 'his most joyful hope would have been realised,' meaning by that that when I saw that Letitia loved me I might have grown to love her, and we should have been married. I said, I remember, that it might have been, for he seemed to expect something like that from me, and I said it to console him. But it was not true; I could never have loved Letitia except as a sister."

"Did your guardian know the name of the poor girl you have lost?"

"O, yes. He met us first when we were walking together, and I introduced him. We had almost a quarrel, my guardian and I, some time afterwards. He said that Miss Melladew was beneath me, and that it would be better if I married in my own station in life. I was hurt and angry, and I begged him to retract his words. Beneath me! She was as far above me as the highest lady in the land could have been. She was the best, the brightest, the purest girl in the world. And I have lost her! I have lost her! What hope is there left to me now?"

He covered his face with his hands, and I waited till he was calm before I spoke again.

"In my hearing," I then said, "you have twice made a remark which struck me as strange. It was to the effect that you would not allow your guardian to give you any more opiates."

"He gave me one last Friday night before I went to bed – on the night my poor Lizzie was killed. I was excited, because I think I told you, sir, that it was decided between Lizzie and me that I should go to her father's house on Sunday, to ask permission to pay my addresses openly to her. Till then I was not to see her again, and that made me restless. My guardian was anxious about me, though he did not know the cause of my restlessness and excitement. To please him I took the opiate, and slept soundly till late in the morning; and when I woke, sir – when I woke and went out to buy a present for Lizzie, which I intended to take to Lizzie on Sunday, almost the first thing I heard—"

He quite broke down here, and a considerable time elapsed before he was sufficiently recovered to continue the conversation.

"Supposing," I said, "that this dreadful event had not occurred, and that you and poor Lizzie had been happily married, would you have continued to give your guardian the income he had enjoyed so long?"

"I do not know – I cannot say. Perhaps not; although I never considered the question. But on the day that I left his house for the home I dreamt and hoped would be mine, the home in which Lizzie and I would have lived happily together. I should have given him something handsome, and I am sure I should always have been his friend. I ought not, perhaps, now that we have gone so far, to conceal anything from you."

"Indeed you ought not. Tell me everything; it may help me."

"I am sure," said the young fellow, with deep feeling, "that he did not mean it, and that he said it only to comfort me. But it made me mad. He hinted that my poor Lizzie could not have been true to me, that she must have had another lover, whom she was in the habit of meeting late at night. If any other man had dared to say as much I would have killed him. But my guardian meant no harm, and when he saw how he had wounded me, he begged my pardon humbly. I am sure, I am sure he repented that he had breathed a suspicion against my poor girl!"

"Pardon me," I said, "for asking you a question which, in any other circumstances, would not cross my lips; but it will be as well for me to put it to you. You yourself had no appointment with her on that night?"

"No," cried Carton indignantly, "as Heaven is my judge! I never met her, I never proposed to meet her, at such an hour!"

"I am certain of it. And yet – receive this calmly, if you can – and yet she must have gone out late on that night for some purpose or other."

"There is the mystery," said Carton mournfully, "and I have thought and thought about it without being able to find a key to it. There must have been a trap set for her – a devilish trap to ensnare her."

"I think so myself. Otherwise it is not likely she would have left her home, as she must have done, secretly. Now, a word or two about Mrs. Dowsett and Letitia."

"When you woke up on Saturday morning you found that they had gone to Margate?"

"Yes."

"Did you know on the day before that they were going?"

"No, nothing was said about it. It was quite sudden."

"Was Mrs. Dowsett or her daughter ill? Did they go into the country for their health?"

"Not to my knowledge."

"Were they in the habit of going away suddenly?"

"O, no; they had never done so before."

"What explanation did your guardian give?"

"He said that Letitia had been suffering in secret for some time, and that her mother thought a change would do her good."

"Did he tell you where they had gone to?"

"No, he did not mention the place. I learnt it from one of the servants."

"So that afterwards he was forced to be frank with you?"

"I don't understand you."

"Reflect. When you rose on Saturday morning you found that Mrs. Dowsett and her daughter had gone away suddenly. You knew nothing at that moment of poor Lizzie's death, and therefore had nothing to trouble you. Did it not strike you as strange that your guardian did not mention the part of the country they had gone to? Or if, your mind being greatly occupied with the arranged interview with Mr. and Mrs. Melladew on the following day, you did not then think it strange that your guardian said nothing of Margate – do you not think so now?"

"Yes," answered Carton thoughtfully, "I do think so now."

"How did you learn that Mrs. Dowsett was stopping at 28 Athelstan Road?"

"By accident. My guardian opened a letter this morning, and a piece of paper dropped from it. I picked it up, and as I gave it to him I saw 28 Athelstan Road written on it. 'Is that where Mrs. Dowsett and Letitia are stopping?' I asked; and he answered, 'Yes.'"

"So that it was not directly through him that you learnt the address?"

"No; but I don't see that it is of any importance."

It was not my cue to enter into an argument, therefore I did not reply to this remark. I had gained from Carton information which, lightly as he regarded it, I deemed of the highest importance. There was, however, still something more which

I desired to speak of, but which I scarcely knew how to approach. After a little reflection I made a bold plunge.

"Is your fortune under your own control?"

"Yes."

"Do you keep a large balance at your bank?"

"Pretty fair; but just now it does not amount to much. Still, if you want any—"

"I do not want any. Am I right in conjecturing that there is a special reason for your balance being small just now?"

"There *is* a special reason. On Saturday morning, before I left home, I drew a large cheque—"

"Which you gave to your guardian."

"How do you know that?" asked Carton, in a tone of surprise.

"It was but a guess. What was the amount of the cheque?"

"Two thousand pounds."

"Payable to 'order' or 'bearer'?"

"To 'bearer.' It was for two investments which Mr. Dowsett recommended. That was the reason for the cheque being made payable to 'bearer,' to enable my guardian to pay it to two different firms. He said both the investments would turn out splendidly, but it matters very little to me now whether they do or not. All the money in the world will not bring happiness to me now that my poor Lizzie is dead."

"Do you know whether your guardian cashed the cheque?"

"I do not; I haven't asked him anything about it. I could think only of one thing."

"I can well imagine it. Thank you for answering my questions so clearly. By and by you may know why I asked them."

These words had hardly passed my lips before Devlin, Carton, and I were thrown violently against each other. The shock was great, but fortunately we were not hurt. Screams of pain from adjoining carriages proclaimed that this was not the case with other passengers. The train was dragged with erratic force for a considerable distance, and then came to a sudden standstill.

"We had best get out," said Devlin, who was the first to recover.

We followed the sensible advice, and, upon emerging from the carriage, discovered that other carriages were overturned, and that the line was blocked. Happily, despite the screams of the frightened passengers, the injuries they had met with were slight, and when all were safely got out we stood along the line, gazing helplessly at each other. Devlin, however, was an exception; he was the only perfectly composed person amongst us.

"It is unfortunate," he said, with a certain maliciousness in his voice; "we are not halfway to Margate. The best laid schemes are liable to come to grief. If Mr. Kenneth Dowsett knew of this, he would rejoice."

It was with intense anxiety that I made inquiries of the guard whether the accident would delay us long. The guard answered that he could not say yet, but that to all appearance we should be delayed two or three hours. I received this information with dismay. It would upon that calculation be midnight before we reached our destination. I considered time so precious that I would have given every shilling in my pocket to have been at that moment in Margate.

"Take it philosophically," said Devlin, at my elbow, "and be thankful that your bones are not broken. It will but prolong the hunt, which, I promise you, shall in the end be successful."

I looked at him almost gratefully for this speculative crumb of comfort, and there was real humour in the smile with which he met my gaze.

"Behold me in another character," he said; "Devlin the Consoler. But you have laid me under an obligation, my dear sir, which I am endeavouring to repay. Your conversation with that unhappy young man" – pointing to Carton, who stood at a little distance from us – "was truly interesting. You have mistaken your vocation; you would have made a first-class detective."

To add to the discomfiture of the situation it began to rain heavily. I felt it would be foolish, and a waste of power, to fret and fume, and I therefore endeavoured to profit by Devlin's advice to take it philosophically. A number of men were now at work setting things straight. They worked with a will, but the guard's prognostication proved correct. It was nearly eleven o'clock before we started again, and past midnight when we arrived at Margate. It was pitch dark, and the furious wind drove the pelting rain into our faces.

"A wild night at sea," cried Devlin, with a kind of exultation in his voice (though this may have been my fancy); he had to speak very loud to make himself heard. "You can do nothing till the morning, and very little then if the storm lasts. Do you know Margate at all?"

"No," I shouted despondently.

"Do you?" asked Devlin, addressing Carton.

"I've never been here before," replied Carton.

"There's a decent hotel not far off," said Devlin: "the Nayland Rock. We'll knock them up, and get beds there. Cling tight to me if you don't want your bones broken. Steady now, steady!"

We had to cling tightly to him, for we could not see a yard before us. Devlin pulled us along, singing some strange wild song at the top of his voice. We were a long time making those in the hotel hear us, but the door was opened at last, and we were admitted. There was only one vacant room in the hotel, but fortunately it contained two beds. To this room we were conducted, and then came the question of settling three persons in the two beds. Devlin solved the difficulty by pulling the counterpanes off, and extending himself full length upon the floor.

"This will do for me," he said, wrapping himself up in the counterpanes. "I've had worse accommodation in my travels through the world. I've slept in the bush, with the sky for a roof; I've slept in the hollow of a tree, with wild beasts howling round me; I've slept on billiard-tables and under them, with a thousand rats running over me and a score of other wanderers. Goodnight, comrades."

Anxiety did not keep me awake; I was tired out, and slept well. When we arose in the morning all signs of the storm had fled. The sun was shining brightly, and a soft warm air flowed through the open window.

XXVI

ANOTHER STRANGE AND UNEXPECTED DISCOVERY

The first thing to be done, after partaking of a hurried breakfast, was to arrange our programme. Carton suggested that we should all go together to Athelstan Road to see his guardian, and I had some difficulty in prevailing upon him to forego this plan. We spoke together quite openly in the presence of Devlin, who, for the most part, contented himself with listening to the discussion.

"Evidently," said Carton, "you have suspicions against my guardian, and it is only fair that he should be made acquainted with them."

"He shall be made acquainted with them," I replied, "but it must be in the way and at the time I deem best. I hold you to your promise to be guided by me."

Carton nodded discontentedly. "I am to stop here and do nothing, I suppose," he said.

"That is how you will best assist me," I said. "If you are seen at present by Mr. Dowsett, you will ruin everything. You shall not, however, be quite idle. Have you your cheque-book with you?"

"Yes," he said, producing it.

"Let me look at the block of the cheque for the two thousand pounds you drew on Saturday morning, payable to bearer, and gave to Mr. Dowsett."

"It is the last cheque I drew," said Carton, handing me the book.

I glanced at it, saw that the bank was the National Provincial Bank of England, and the number of the cheque 134,178. Then I obtained a telegraph form, and at my instruction Carton wrote the following telegram:

"To the Manager, National Provincial Bank of England, 112 Bishopsgate Street, London. Has my cheque for two thousand pounds (No. 134,178), drawn by me on Saturday, and made payable to bearer, been cashed, and how was it paid, in notes or gold? Reply paid. Urgent. Waiting here for answer. From Richard Carton, Nayland Rock Hotel, Margate."

"I will take this myself to the telegraph-office," I said, "and you will wait here for the answer. I will be back as quickly as possible, but it is likely I may be absent for an hour or more."

With that I left him, Devlin accompanying me at my request.

I could have sent the telegram from the railway station, but I chose to send it from the local post-office, for the reason that I expected to receive there a telegram from my wife, whom I had instructed to wire to me, before eight o'clock, whether there was anything fresh in the London newspapers concerning the murder of Lizzie Melladew. I mentioned this to Devlin, and he said,

"You omit nothing; it is a pleasure to work with you. Command me in any way you please. My turn, perhaps, will come by and by."

It was early morning, and our way lay along the Marine Parade, every house in which was either a public or a boarding house. From every basement in the row, as we walked on, ascended one uniform odour of the cooking of bacon and eggs, which caused Devlin to humorously remark that when bacon and eggs ceased to be the breakfast of the average Englishman, the decay of England's greatness would commence. All along the line this familiar odour accompanied us.

At the post-office I found my wife's telegram awaiting me. It was to the effect that there was nothing new in the papers concerning the murder. The criminal was still at large, and the police appeared to have failed in obtaining a clue. I despatched Carton's telegram to the London bank, and then we proceeded to Athelstan Road, and soon found the house we were in search of. I had decided upon my plan of operations: Devlin was not to appear; he was to stand at some distance from the house, and only to come forward if I called him. I was to knock and inquire for Mr. Dowsett, and explain to him that, not feeling well, I had run down to Margate for the day. Carton had given me his guardian's address, and had asked me to inquire whether Mr. Dowsett would be absent from London for any length of time, intending, if such was the case, to join Mr. Dowsett and his family in the country. Then I was to trust to chance and to anything I observed how next to proceed. The whole invention was as lame as well could be, but I could not think of a better. It was only when decided action was necessary that I felt how powerless I was. All that I had to depend upon was a slender and mysterious thread of conjecture.

I knocked at the door, and of the servant who opened it I inquired if Mr. Dowsett was up yet.

"O, yes, sir," replied the girl. "Up and gone, all of 'em."

"Up and gone, all of them!" I exclaimed.

"Yes, sir. Had breakfast at half-past six, and went away directly afterwards."

"Do you know where to?"

"No, sir. O, here's missus."

The landlady came forward. "Do you want rooms, sir?"

"Not at present. I came to see Mr. Dowsett."

"Gone away, sir; him and the three ladies."

"So your servant informed me; but I thought I should be certain to find him here. Stop. What did you say? Mr. Dowsett and the three ladies? You mean the two ladies?"

"I mean three," said the landlady, looking sharply at me. "They only came on Saturday; Mr. Dowsett came yesterday. You must excuse me, sir; there's the dining-room bell and the drawing-room bell ringing all together."

"A moment, I beg," I said, slipping half-a-crown into her hand. "Do you know where they have gone to?"

"No; they didn't tell me. They were in a hurry to catch a train; but I don't know what train, and don't know where to."

Her manner proclaimed that she not only did not know, but did not care.

"They had some boxes with them?" I said.

"Yes, two. I can't wait another minute. I never did see such a impatient gentleman as the dining-rooms."

"Only one more question," I said, forcibly detaining her. "Did they drive to the station?"

"Yes; they had a carriage. Please let me go, sir."

"Do you know the man who drove them? Do you know the number of the carriage?"

"Haven't the slightest idea," said the landlady; and, freeing herself from my grasp, she ran down to her kitchen.

I stepped into the street with a feeling of mortification. Mr. Kenneth Dowsett had given me the slip again. Rejoining Devlin, I related to him what had passed.

"What are you going to do next?" he asked.

"I am puzzled," I replied, "and hardly know what to do."

"That is not like you," said Devlin. "Come, I will assist you. Mr. Kenneth Dowsett seems to be in a hurry. The more reason for spirit and increased vigilance on our part. Observe, I say our part. I am growing interested in this case, and am curious to see the end of it. If Mr. Dowsett has gone back to London, we must follow him there. If he has gone to some other place, we must follow him to some other place."

"But how to find that out?"

"He was driven to the station in a carriage. We must get hold of the driver. At present we are ignorant whether he has gone by the South-Eastern or the London, Chatham, and Dover. We will go and inquire at the cab-ranks."

But although we spent fully an hour and a half in asking questions of every driver of a carriage we saw, we could ascertain no news of the carriage which had driven Mr. Dowsett and his family from Athelstan Road. I was in despair, and was about to give up the search and return disconsolately to the Nayland Rock, when a barefooted boy ran up to me, and asked whether I wasn't looking for "the cove wot drove a party from Athelstan Road."

"Yes," I said excitedly. "Do you know him?"

"O, I knows him," said the boy. "Bill Foster he is. I 'elped him up with the boxes. There was one little box the gent wouldn't let us touch. There was somethink 'eavy in it, and the gent give me a copper. Thank yer, sir."

He was about to scuttle off with the sixpence I gave him, when I seized him, not by the collar, because he had none on, but by the neck where the collar should have been.

"Not so fast. There's half-a-crown more for you if you take me to Bill Foster at once."

"Can't do that, sir; don't know where he is; but I'll find 'im for yer."

"Very good. How many persons went away in Bill Foster's carriage?"

"There was the gent and one-two-three women – two young 'uns and a old 'un."

"You're quite sure?"

"I'll take my oath on it."

"Now look here? Do you see these five shillings? They're yours if you bring Bill Foster to me at the Nayland Rock in less than half-an-hour."

"You ain't kidding, sir?"

"Not at all. The money's yours if you do what I tell you."

"All right, sir? I'll do it."

"And tell Bill Foster there's half-a-sovereign waiting for him at the Nayland Rock; but he mustn't lose a minute."

With an intelligent nod the boy scampered off, and we made our way quickly back to the hotel, where Richard Carton was impatiently waiting us.

"Did you see him?" he asked eagerly.

"No," I replied, "he went away early this morning."

"Where to?"

"I hope to learn that presently. Have you received an answer to your telegram?"

"No, not yet. There's the telegraph messenger."

The lad was mounting the steps of the hotel. We followed him, and obtained the buff-coloured envelope, addressed to "Richard Carton, Nayland Rock Hotel, Margate," which he delivered to a waiter. Carton tore open the envelope, read the message, and handed it to me. The information it contained was that cheque 134,178, for two thousand pounds, signed by Richard Carton, was cashed across the counter on Saturday morning; that the gentleman who presented it demanded that it should be paid in gold; that as this was a large amount to be so paid the cashier had asked the gentleman to sign his name at the back of the cheque, notwithstanding that it was payable to bearer, and that the signature was that of Kenneth Dowsett.

"Do you think there is anything strange in that?" I asked.

"It does seem strange," replied Carton thoughtfully.

I made a rapid mental calculation, and said, "Two thousand sovereigns in gold weigh forty pounds. A heavy weight for a man to carry away with him." Carton did not reply, but I saw that, for the first time, his suspicions were aroused. "You told me," I continued, "that Mrs. Dowsett and her daughter Letitia went away from their house on Saturday morning early."

"So my guardian informed me."

"Was any other lady stopping with them?"

"I did not understand so from my guardian."

"Did they have any particular lady friend whom, for some reason or other, they wished to take with them to the seaside?"

"Not to my knowledge."

"You can think of no one?"

"Indeed, I cannot."

"It is your belief that only two ladies left the house?'

"Yes, it is my belief."

"But," I said, "Mrs. Dowsett took not only her daughter Letitia with her, but another lady, a young lady, as well; and the three, in company with your guardian, left Margate suddenly this morning. I have ascertained this positively. Now, who is this young lady of whom you have no knowledge?" He passed his hand across his forehead, and gazed at me with a dawning terror in his eyes. "Shall I tell you what is in my mind?"

"Yes."

"If," I said, speaking slowly and impressively, "the theory I have formed is correct – and I believe it is – the young lady is Mary Melladew, poor Lizzie's sister."

"Good God!" cried Carton. "What makes you think that?"

XXVII

WE TRACK MR. KENNETH DOWSETT TO BOULOGNE

"It would occupy too long a time," I replied, "to make my theory thoroughly comprehensible to you. Besides," I added, glancing at Devlin, "it is a theory strangely born and strangely built up, and, in all likelihood, you would reject the most important parts of it as incredible and impossible. Therefore, we will not waste time in explaining or discussing it. Sufficient for us if we succeed in tracing this dreadful mystery to its roots and in bringing the murderer to justice. If I do not mistake, here comes the man I am waiting for."

It was, indeed. Bill Foster, pioneered by the sharp lad who had engaged to find him.

"Here he is, sir," said the boy, holding out his hand, half-eagerly, half-doubtfully.

"Your name is Foster," I said, addressing the man.

"That's me," said Bill Foster.

"You drove a party from Athelstan Road early this morning?"

"Yes."

I counted five shillings into the boy's outstretched hand, and he scampered away in great delight.

"There's half-a-sovereign for you," I said to Bill Foster, "if you answer correctly a few questions."

"About the party I drove from Athelstan Road?" he asked.

"My questions will refer to them. You seem to hesitate."

"The fact is," said Bill Foster, "the gentleman gave me a florin over my fare to keep my mouth shut."

"Only a fifth of what I offer you," I said.

"Make it a sovereign," suggested Devlin.

"I've no objection," I said.

"All right," said Bill Foster; "fire away."

"The gentleman bribed you to keep silence respecting his movements?" I asked.

"It must have been for that," replied Bill Foster.

"Proving," I observed, "that he must have had some strong reason for secrecy."

"That's got nothing to do with me," remarked Bill Foster.

"Of course not. What you've got to do is to earn the sovereign. Who engaged you for the job?"

"The gentleman himself. I wasn't out with my trap so early, and someone must have told him where I live. Anyways, he comes at a quarter-past six, and knocks me up, and says there's a good job waiting for me at 28 Athelstan Road, if I'd come at once. I says, 'All right,' and I puts my horse to, and drives there. I got to the house at ten minutes to seven, and I drives the party to the London, Chatham, and Dover."

"How many were in the party?"

"Four. The gentleman, a middle-aged lady, and two young 'uns."

"About what ages were the young ladies?"

"Can't quite say. They wore veils; but I should reckon from eighteen to twenty-two. That's near enough."

"What luggage was there?"

"Two trunks, a small box, and some other little things they took care of themselves."

"You had charge of the two trunks?"

"Yes."

"And of the small box?"

"O, no; the gentleman wouldn't let it out of his hands. I offered to help him with it, but he wouldn't let me touch it."

"That surprised you?"

"Well, yes, because it was uncommon heavy. If it was filled with gold he couldn't have been more careful of it."

"Perhaps it was," I said, turning slightly to Richard Carton.

"It was heavy enough. Why, he could hardly carry it."

"Did either of the ladies appear anxious about it?"

"Yes, the middle-aged one. When I saw them so particular, I said, said I – to myself, you know – I shouldn't mind having that myself."

"When the gentleman told you to drive to the London, Chatham, and Dover station, did he say what train he wished to catch?"

"No, but I found out the train they went by. It was the down train for Ramsgate, 7.31."

"They reached the station some time before it started?"

"Yes, twenty minutes before. After the gentleman took his tickets he came from the platform two or three times and looked at me. 'What are you waiting for?' he asked the last time. 'For a fare,' I answered. 'Look here,' he said, 'if anybody asks you any questions about me, don't answer them.' 'Why shouldn't I?' I asked. It was then he pulled out the florin. 'O, very well,' I said; 'it's no business of mine.' But I didn't go away till the train started with them in it."

"Do you know whether they intended to stop in Margate?"

"I should say not. As I drove 'em to the station, I heard the gentleman speak to the middle-aged lady – his wife, I suppose – about the boat for Boulogne."

I gave a start of vexation; Devlin smiled; Carton was following the conversation with great attention.

"Do you know what boat?"

"The Sir Walter Raleigh. The gentleman had one of the bills in his hand, and was looking at it. He said to the lady, 'We shall be in plenty of time.'"

"Do you know at what time the boat starts from Ramsgate for Boulogne?"

"Leaves the harbour at half-past nine, but is generally half an hour late."

I looked at my watch. It was just eleven o'clock.

"Is there any chance," I asked, "of this boat being delayed?"

"Why should it? The weather's fair."

"Is there any other boat starting for Boulogne this morning?"

"None. There's the Sir Walter Raleigh from Ramsgate, and sometimes the India from here; but the India don't go today."

"Could we hire a boat from here?"

"You might, but it would be risky, and would cost a lot of money. Then, there's no saying when you would get there. It's a matter of between forty and fifty miles, and the steamers take about five hours getting across; sometimes a little less, generally a little more. There's no depending upon 'em. Look here. You're going to behave to me liberal. You want to follow the party I drove from Athelstan Road this morning."

"Show me the way to get to Boulogne today," I said, "and I'll give you another half-sovereign."

"Practical creature!" murmured Devlin. "In human dealings there is but one true touchstone."

"Spoke like a real gentleman," said Bill Foster to me. "What time is it?"

"Five minutes past eleven."

"Wait here; I sha'n't be gone but a few minutes. Get everything ready to start directly I come back."

His trap was standing at the corner of Royal Crescent. He ran out, jumped on the box, and was gone. I called to the waiter, and in three minutes the hotel bill was paid, and we were ready.

During Bill Foster's absence I said to Carton,

"Do you make anything of all this?"

"It looks," replied Carton, "as if my guardian was running away."

"To my mind there's not a doubt of it. Have you any idea what that little box he would not let out of his charge contains?"

"The two thousand sovereigns he obtained from the bank," said Carton, in a tone of inquiry.

"Exactly. I tell you now plainly that I am positive Mr. Kenneth Dowsett is implicated in the murder of your poor girl."

Carton set his teeth in great agitation. "If he is! if he is!" he said; but he could say no more.

Bill Foster was back.

"There's a train to Folkestone," he cried, "the South-Eastern line, at 11.47. You can catch it easily. If there's no boat handy from Folkestone to Boulogne, you'll be able to hire one there. The steamers take two hours going across. You can get there in four. Train arrives at Folkestone at 1.27. By six o'clock you can be in Boulogne. Jump into my trap, gentlemen."

We jumped in, and were driven to the station. His information was correct. I gave him thirty shillings, and he departed in high glee. Then we took tickets for Folkestone, and arrived there at a quarter to two.

There was no steamer going, but with little difficulty we arranged to get across. The passage took longer than four hours – it took six. At nine o'clock at night we were in Boulogne.

I cannot speak an intelligible sentence in French. Carton was too agitated to take the direction of affairs.

"Do you know where we can stop?" I asked of Devlin. "Have you ever been here before?"

"My dear sir," said Devlin, "I have travelled all over the world, and I know Boulogne by heart. There's a little out-of-the-way hotel, the Hôtel de Poilly, in Rue de l'AmiralBruix, that will suit us as though it were built for us."

"Let us get there at once," I said.

He called a fly, and in a very short time we entered the courtyard of the Hotel de Poilly. There we made arrangements with the jolly, comfortable-looking landlady, and then I looked at Carton, and he looked at me. The helplessness of our situation struck us both forcibly.

"Who is in command?" asked Devlin suddenly.

"You," I replied, as by an inspiration.

"Good," said Devlin. "I accept the office. From this moment you are under my orders. Remain you here; I go to reconnoitre."

"You will return?" I said.

"My dear sir," said Devlin airily, "it is too late now to doubt my integrity. I will return."

"For God's sake," said Carton, when Devlin was gone, "who is this man who seems to divine everything, to know everything, and whom nothing disturbs? Sometimes when he looks at me I feel that he is exercising over me a terrible fascination."

"I cannot answer you," I said. "Be satisfied with the knowledge that it is through him we have so far succeeded, and that, in my belief, it will be through him that the murderer will be tracked down. The world is full of mysteries, and that man is not the least of them."

It wanted an hour to midnight when Devlin returned. In his inscrutable face I read no sign of success or failure; but the first words he spoke afforded me infinite relief.

"I have seen him," he said. "Let us go out and talk. Walls have ears."

The river Liane was but a short distance from the hotel, and we strolled along the bank in silence, Devlin, contrary to my expectation, not uttering a word for many minutes. He had lit a cigar, and Carton had accepted one from him; I refused to smoke, having too vivid a remembrance of the cigar I had smoked in Fanny Lemon's house, and its effect upon me. At length Devlin said to Carton:

"You appear sleepy."

"I am," said the young man.

"You had best go to bed," said Devlin; "nothing can be done tonight."

Carton, assenting, would have returned to the hotel alone, saying he could find the way, but I insisted that we should accompany him thither. I had heard that Boulogne was not the safest place in the world for strangers on a dark night. Having seen Carton to his room, we returned to the river's bank. Had Carton been in possession of his full senses he would doubtless have objected, but he was dead asleep when he entered his bedroom, Devlin's cigar having affected him as the one I smoked had affected me.

"He encumbers us," said Devlin, looking out upon the dark river. "I have discovered where Mr. Dowsett is lodging, and were our young friend informed of the address he might rush there, and spoil all. We happen to be in luck, if you believe in such a quality as luck. I do not; but I use the term out of compliment to you. Mr. Dowsett's quarters are in the locality of the Rue de la Paix, and, singularly enough, are situated over a barber's shop. Things go in runs, do they not? Nothing but barbers. I do not return with you to the hotel tonight."

"What do you mean?" I asked, startled by this information.

"The proprietor of the barber's shop over which Mr. Kenneth Dowsett is sleeping – but, perhaps, not sleeping, for a sword is hanging above his head, and he may be gazing at the phantom in terror – say, then, over which he is lying, is an agreeable person. I have struck up an acquaintance with him, and, by arrangement, shall be in his saloon tomorrow, to attend to any persons who may present themselves. Mr. Dowsett will probably need the razor and the brush. I can easily account for my appearance in Boulogne; I have come to see my friend and brother. Mr. Dowsett, unsuspecting – for what connection can he trace between me and Lizzie Melladew? – will place himself in my hands. He has told me that there is not my equal;

he may find that it is so. In order that I may not miss him I go to the house tonight. Early in the morning come you, alone, to the Rue de la Paix. You can ride to the foot of the hill, there alight, and on the right-hand side, a third of the way up, you will see my new friend's establishment. I will find you a snug corner from which you may observe and hear, yourself unseen, all that passes. Are you satisfied now that I am keeping faith with you?"

"Indeed, you are proving it," I replied.

"Give me no more credit than I deserve," said Devlin. "It is simply that I keep a promise. In the fulfilment of this promise – both in the spirit and to the letter, my dear sir – I may tomorrow unfold to you a wonder. It is my purpose to compel the man we have pursued to himself reveal all that he knows of Lizzie Melladew. Perhaps it will be as well for you to take down in writing what passes between us. Accept it from me that there are unseen forces and unseen powers in this world, so rich in sin, of which few men dream. See those shadows moving on the water – are they not like living spirits? The dark river itself, had it a tongue, could appal you. On such nights as this are secret crimes committed by devils who bear the shape of men. What kind of being is that who smiles in your face, who presses your hand, who speaks pleasant words to you, and harbours all the while in what is called his heart a fell design towards the execution of which he moves without one spark of compassion? I don't complain of him, my dear sir; on the contrary" – and here, although I could not see Devlin's face, I could fancy a sinister smile overspreading it – "I rather delight in him. It proves him to be what he is – and he is but a type of innumerable others. Your innocent ones are arrogant in the vaunting of their goodness; your ambitious ones glory in their successes which bring ruin to their brethren; your kings and emperors appropriate Providence, and do not even pay him a shilling for the conscription. A grand world, and grandly peopled! The man who glories in sin compels my admiration; but this one whom we are hunting is a coward and a sneak. He shall meet his doom!"

As he ceased speaking he vanished; I can find no other word to express the effect his sudden disappearance had upon me. Whether he intended to create a dramatic surprise I cannot say, but, certainly, he was no longer by my side. With some difficulty I found my way alone back to the Hotel de Poilly, where Carton was fast asleep.

XXVIII

THE TRANCE AND THE REVELATION

Of all the strange experiences I have narrated in connection with Devlin, that which awaited me on the following morning was the most startling and inexplicable. Prevailing with difficulty upon Richard Carton to remain at the hotel until I either came to or sent for him, I drove to the foot of the Rue de la Paix, as I was instructed to do. I took the precaution to hire the driver of the fly by the hour, and desired him to stop where I alighted until I needed him. I was impelled to this course by a feeling that I might possibly require some person to take a message to Carton or bring him to the Rue de la Paix. I found the barber's shop easily, and could scarcely refrain from uttering a loud exclamation at the sight of Mr. Kenneth Dowsett sitting in a barber's chair, and Devlin standing over him, leisurely at work. Devlin, with his finger at his lips, pointed to a table in a corner of the shop, at which I seated myself in obedience to the silent command. On the table were writing materials and paper, and on a sheet of this paper was written: "You are late. I have thrown Mr. Dowsett into a trance. He will reveal all he knows. I will compel him to do so. Take down in writing what transpires."

My heart throbbed violently as I prepared myself for the task.

Devlin: "Do you know where you are?"

Mr. Dowsett: "Yes, in Boulogne."

Devlin: "Where were you yesterday?"

Mr. Dowsett: "In Margate."

Devlin: "Where were you on Friday last?"

Mr. Dowsett: "At home, in London."

Devlin: "Recall the occurrences of that day?"

Mr. Dowsett: "I do so."

Devlin: "At what hour did you rise?"

Mr. Dowsett: "At nine o'clock."

Devlin: "Who were present at the breakfast-table?"

Mr. Dowsett: "My wife and daughter, and Richard Carton."

Devlin: "Was anything relating to the engagement of Richard Carton and Lizzie Melladew said at the breakfast-table?"

Mr. Dowsett: "Nothing."

Devlin: "Was there anything in your mind in relation to it?"

Mr. Dowsett: "Yes. I had a plan to carry out, and was thinking of it."

Devlin: "In what way did you put the plan into execution?"

Mr. Dowsett: "When breakfast was over, I went to my private room and locked the door. Then I sat down and wrote a letter."

Devlin: "To whom?"

Mr. Dowsett: "To Lizzie Melladew."

Devlin: "What did you write?"

Mr. Dowsett: "A heartbroken woman implores you to meet her tonight at eleven o'clock in Victoria Park, and, so that she may recognise you, begs you to wear a bunch of white daisies in your belt. She will wear the same, so that you may recognise her. The life and welfare of Mr. Richard Carton hangs upon this meeting. If you fail, a dreadful fate awaits him, which you can avert. As you value his happiness and your own, come."

Devlin: "What did you do with the letter?"

Mr. Dowsett: "I addressed it to Miss Lizzie Melladew, at her place of business in Baker Street, and posted it at the Charing Cross Post-office."

Devlin: "How did you know she worked there?"

Mr. Dowsett: "I learnt it from my ward, Richard Carton."

Devlin: "Did you disguise your handwriting?"

Mr. Dowsett: "Yes; I wrote it in a feminine hand."

Devlin: "What was your object in writing the letter?"

Mr. Dowsett: "I was determined that Richard Carton should not marry Lizzie Melladew."

Devlin: "Why?"

Mr. Dowsett: "I had all along arranged that he should marry my daughter Letitia."

Devlin: "How did you propose to break off the match between your ward and Lizzie Melladew?"

Mr. Dowsett: "My plans were not entirely clear to myself. I intended to appeal to the young woman, and to invent some disreputable story to make her suspect that he was false to her. If that failed, then—"

Devlin: "Proceed. Then?"

Mr. Dowsett: "I was resolved to go any lengths, to do anything to prevent the marriage."

Devlin: "Even murder."

Mr. Dowsett: "I did not think of that – I would not think of it."

Devlin: "But you did think of it. You could not banish that idea from your mind?"

Mr. Dowsett: "I could not, though I tried. It crept in the whole of the day. I could not help seeing the scene. Night – the park – the young woman with the bunch of white daisies in her belt stained with blood."

Devlin: "Those pictures were in your mind, and you could not banish them?"

Mr. Dowsett: "I could not."

Devlin: "There were other reasons for preventing the marriage than your wish that Richard Carton should marry your daughter?"

Mr. Dowsett: "There were."

Devlin: "What were they?"

Mr. Dowsett: "If he married Lizzie Melladew, I should no longer enjoy the income I had received for so many years. I looked upon it as mine. I could not live without it. We should have been beggared – disgraced as well. I had forged my ward's name to bills, and if he married out of my family there would have been exposure, and I might have found myself in a felon's dock. If he married my daughter this would not occur. I was safe so long as I could keep my hold upon him."

Devlin: "Did your wife and daughter know this?"

Mr. Dowsett: "My daughter knew nothing of it. My wife suspected it."

Devlin: "Did she know that you contemplated murder?"

Mr. Dowsett: "She did not."

Devlin: "Why did you give Richard Carton a sleeping draught on that night?"

Mr. Dowsett: "In order that he might sleep soundly, and not discover that I left the house late."

Devlin: "Were your wife and daughter asleep when you left your house?"

Mr. Dowsett: "They were abed. I do not know whether they were asleep."

Devlin: "You took a knife with you?"

Mr. Dowsett: "I did."

Devlin: "Where did you obtain it?"

Mr. Dowsett: "It was a large clasp knife I had had for years. I found it in a private drawer."

Devlin: "You went to the private drawer for the purpose of finding it?"

Mr. Dowsett: "I did."

Devlin: "Did anyone see you leave the house?"

Mr. Dowsett: "No one."

Devlin: "Did you walk or ride to Victoria Park?"

Mr. Dowsett: "I walked."

Devlin: "To avoid suspicion?"

Mr. Dowsett: "Yes."

Devlin: "When you arrived at the Park did you have any difficulty in finding Miss Melladew?"

Mr. Dowsett: "I soon found her."

Devlin: "What did you do then?"

Mr. Dowsett: "I made an appeal to her."

Devlin: "Did she listen to you quietly?"

Mr. Dowsett: "No. She taunted me with having tricked her by writing an anonymous letter in a disguised hand."

Devlin: "Go on."

Mr. Dowsett: "I told her it was the only way I could obtain a private interview with her. I invented a scandalous story about my ward. She said she did not believe it, and that she would expose me to him. She told me that I was infamous, and that it was her belief I had been systematically practising deceit upon my ward, and that she would not be surprised to discover that I had been robbing him. 'Tomorrow he shall see you in your true colours,' she said. I was maddened. If she carried out her intention I knew that I was a ruined and disgraced man. 'That tomorrow will never come!' I cried. The knife was in my hand. I scarcely know how it came there, and do not remember opening the blade. 'That tomorrow will come!' she retorted. 'It shall not!' I cried; and I stabbed her to the heart. She uttered but one cry, and fell down dead."

Devlin: "What did you do after that?"

Mr. Dowsett: "I hastened away, taking the knife with me. I chose the darkest paths. Suddenly I came upon a young woman sitting upon a bench, reclining against the back. I saw her face, and was rooted to the spot in sudden fear. She did not stir. Recovering, I crept softly towards her, and found that she was asleep. Leaving her there, I hastened back to the woman I had stabbed. I knelt down and looked closely at her. I felt in her pockets; she was quite dead. There were letters in her pockets which I examined, and then – and then—"

Devlin: "And then?"

Mr. Dowsett: "I discovered that the woman I had killed was not Lizzie Melladew!"

XXIX

THE RESCUE

So startled was I by this revelation that I jumped to my feet in a state of uncontrollable agitation. What I should have done I cannot say, but the direction of events was not left in my hands. Simultaneously with my movement of astonishment, a piercing scream rang through the house.

I was standing now by the chair in which Mr. Kenneth Dowsett was sitting in his trance, and I observed a change pass over his face; the scream had pierced the veil in which his waking senses were enshrouded. Devlin also observed this change, and he said to me hurriedly:

"Go upstairs and see what is taking place. Your presence may be needed there, and to one person may be very welcome. I will keep charge over this man."

As I left the room I heard Devlin turn the key in the lock. Rapidly I mounted the stairs, and dashed into a room on the first landing, from which the sound of female voices were issuing. Three women were there; two were strangers to me, but even in that agitating moment I correctly divined that they were Mrs. Dowsett and Letitia; the third, who rushed with convulsive sobs into my open arms, was no other than Lizzie Melladew herself.

"O, thank God, you have come!" she sobbed; "thank God! thank God! Where is Mary? Where is Richard? Take me to them! O, take me to them!"

Mrs. Dowsett was the first to recover herself. "You will remain here," she said sternly to Lizzie; and then, addressing me, "How dare you break into my apartment in this manner?"

"I dare do more than that," I replied, in a voice sterner than her own, and holding the weeping girl close to my heart. "Prepare you to answer for what has been done. I thank God, indeed, that I have arrived in time, perhaps, to prevent another crime. All is discovered."

At these words Mrs. Dowsett shrank back, white and trembling. I did not stop to say more. My first duty was to place Lizzie Melladew in safety; but where? The mental question conveyed its own answer. Where, but in her lover's arms?

"Come," I said to Lizzie. "You are safe now. I am going to take you to Richard Carton. Trust yourself to me."

"I will, I will!" sobbed Lizzie, "Richard is here, then? How thankful I am, how thankful! And Mary, my dear sister, is she here, too?"

I was appalled at this last question. It proved that Lizzie was ignorant of what had occurred. Not daring to answer her, I drew her from the room, and the women I left there made no attempt to prevent me. Swiftly I took my precious charge from the house, and in a very few minutes we were in the carriage which was waiting for me at the foot of the Rue de la Paix. The driver understood the direction I gave him, and we galloped at full speed to the Hotel de Poilly. Without revealing to Lizzie what I knew, I learnt from her before we reached the hotel sufficient to enlighten me as to Mr. Kenneth Dowsett's proceedings, and to confirm my suspicion that it was Mary Melladew who had met her death at that villain's hands. When Lizzie received the anonymous letter which he wrote to her, she took it to her poor sister, who, fearing some plot, prevailed upon her to let her see the anonymous writer in Lizzie's place; and, the better to carry out the plan, the sisters changed dresses, and went together to Victoria Park. Being twins, and bearing so close a resemblance to each other, there was little fear of the change being discovered until at least Mary had ascertained why the meeting was so urgently desired. Leaving Lizzie in a secluded part of the park, Mary proceeded to the rendezvous, with what result Mr. Dowsett's confession has already made clear. Discovering the fatal error he had committed, Mr. Dowsett returned to Lizzie, who, while waiting for her sister, had fallen asleep. Being thoroughly unnerved, he decided that there was only one means of safety before him – flight and the concealment of Lizzie Melladew. The idea of a second murder may have occurred to him, but, villain as he was, he had not the courage to carry it out. He had taken from the dead girl's pocket everything it contained, with the exception of a handkerchief which, in his haste, he overlooked; and upon this handkerchief was marked the name of Lizzie Melladew. He could imitate Richard Carton's writing –as was proved by the forgeries he had already committed – and upon the back of this anonymous letter he wrote in pencil a few words in which Lizzie was implored to trust herself implicitly to Mr. Dowsett, and without question to do as he directed. Signing these words in Richard Carton's name, he awoke Lizzie and gave her the note. Alarmed and agitated as the young girl was, and fearing that some great danger threatened her lover, she, with very little hesitation, allowed herself to be persuaded by Mr. Dowsett, and accompanied him home. "Where is Mary?" she asked. "With our dear Richard," replied Mr. Dowsett; "we shall see them tomorrow, when all will be explained." At home Mr. Dowsett informed his wife of his peril, and the three females left for Margate by an early train in the morning. In Margate Mrs. Dowsett received telegrams signed "Richard Carton," but really sent by her husband, which she showed to Lizzie, and which served in some measure to assist the successful continuation of the scheme by which Lizzie was to be taken out of the country. Meanwhile she was in absolute ignorance of her sister's fate; no newspaper was allowed to reach her hands, nor was she allowed to speak to a soul but Mrs. Dowsett and Letitia. What was eventually to be done with her I cannot say; probably Mr. Dowsett himself had not been able to make up his mind, which was almost entirely occupied by considerations for his own safety.

I did not, of course, learn all this from Lizzie, she being then ignorant of much which I have related, but I have put together what she told me and what I subsequently learnt from Devlin and other sources.

Arriving at the Hotel de Poilly, I succeeded in conveying Lizzie into a private room, and then I sought Richard Carton. I need not set down here in detail the conversation I had with him. Little by little I made him acquainted with the whole truth. Needless to describe his joy when he heard that his beloved girl was alive and safe – joy, tempered with grief at poor Mary's fate. When he was calm enough to be practical, he asked me what was to be done.

"No time must be lost," I said, "in restoring your dear Lizzie to her parents. To you I shall confide her. Leave that monster, your treacherous guardian, to Devlin and me."

It was with difficulty I restrained him from rushing to Lizzie, but I insisted that his movements must be definitely decided upon before he saw her. I called in the assistance of the jolly landlady, and she supplied me with a time-table, from which I ascertained that a boat for Dover left at 12.31, and that it was timed to reach its destination at 3.20. There were numerous trains from Dover to London, and Lizzie would be in her parents' arms before night. Carton joyfully acquiesced in this arrangement, and then I took him in to his dear girl, and, closing the door upon them, left them to themselves. A meeting such as theirs, and under such circumstances, was sacred.

While they were together I wrote two letters – one to my wife, and the other to Mr. Portland – which I intended should be delivered by Carton. I did not intrude upon the happy lovers till the last moment. I found them sitting close together, quite silent, hand clasped in hand, her head upon his breast. I had cautioned him to say nothing of Mary's sad fate, and I saw by the expression upon Lizzie's face that he had obeyed me. After joy would come sorrow; there was time enough for that. Mary had given her life for her sister's; the sacrifice would ever be held in sacred remembrance.

I saw them off by the boat; they waved their handkerchiefs to me, and I thought of the Melladews mourning at home, to whom, at least, one dear child would soon be restored. When the boat was out of sight, I jumped into the carriage, and was driven back to the Rue de la Paix.

XXX

DEVLIN'S LAST SCHEME

I tried the door of the room in which I had left Devlin and Mr. Kenneth Dowsett. It was locked.

"Enter," said Devlin, unlocking the door.

They were both in the room, Devlin smiling and unruffled, Mr. Dowsett in the full possession of his senses, and terribly ill at ease.

He turned like death when he saw me.

"This gentleman," said Devlin, "is angry at being detained by me, and would have resorted to violence if he thought it would serve his purpose. I have waited for your return to decide what to do."

"You shall pay for this," Mr. Dowsett managed to say, "you and your confederate. If there is justice in this world, I will make you smart for your unlawful proceedings."

"There *is* justice in the world," I said calmly, "as you shall find."

He was silent. With a weight of guilt upon his soul, he did not know how to reply to this remark. But he managed presently to ask:

"How long do you intend to detain me?"

"You shall know soon," I said; and, by a gesture, I intimated to Devlin that I wished to confer with him alone.

He accompanied me from the room, and we stood in the passage, keeping guard upon the door, which Devlin locked from the outside.

"There are no means of escape from within," he said. "I have seen to that."

In a low tone I told him what I had done, and he approved.

"The question now is," I said, "what step are we next to take?"

"There lies the difficulty," replied Devlin. "You see my dear sir, we have no evidence upon which to arrest him."

"No evidence!" I cried. "Is there not his own confession of guilt?"

Devlin shook his head. "Spiritual evidence only, my dear sir. Not admissible in any court of law in the world. Impossible to obtain his arrest in a foreign country upon such a slender thread. He might bring the same accusation against us, and we might all be thrown into gaol, and kept there for months. That is not what I bargained for. Our best plan will be to get him back to England; then you can take some practicable step."

"But how to manage that?" I asked.

"It can be managed, I think," said Devlin. "I have a scheme. He knows nothing of the confession he has made. Lizzie Melladew's name has not been mentioned between us. It is only his fears and my strength of will that make him tractable. Before I put my scheme into operation, go upstairs to see if his wife and daughter are in the house. I have my suspicions that they have flown. You will find me here when you come down."

I ran upstairs to the apartments occupied by Mrs. Dowsett. Devlin's suspicions were confirmed. The two women were gone. There were evidences around of a hasty flight, the most pregnant of them being a small box which had been broken open. I judged immediately that this was the box which had contained the two thousand sovereigns; and, indeed, I found two of the sovereigns under a couch, whither they had rolled while the bulk was being taken out. The conclusion I came to was, that the women, frightened that all was discovered, as I had informed them, had broken open the box, and, packing the gold away upon their persons, had taken to flight, leaving Mr. Dowsett to his fate.

I went down to Devlin, and acquainted him with the result of my investigation.

"Quite as I expected," he said. "Let them go for the present. Our concern is with the man inside. I am going to put my scheme into operation. What is the time?"

"Five minutes past two," I replied, looking at my watch.

"In capital time," said Devlin. "Wait you here until half-past two. Then go in to Mr. Dowsett, and apologise to him for the indignity to which he has been subjected. He will fume and threaten; let him. Be you humble and contrite, and say that you are very, very sorry. Throw all the blame upon me: say that I have deceived you, imposed upon you, robbed you – anything that comes to your mind. To me it matters not; it will assist our scheme. There is no fear of Mr. Dowsett not waiting till you go in to him; he is frightened out of his life. Your humble attitude will give him courage; he will think himself safe."

"I cannot imagine," I said, "how this will help us."

"Don't imagine," said Devlin curtly. "Leave all to me. The first thing Mr. Dowsett will do when he finds himself free will be to go up to the rooms in which he left the three women who accompanied him here. Meanwhile, you will keep watch outside the house; but on no account must he see you. Trust to me for the rest."

He had served me so faithfully up to this point that I trusted him unhesitatingly. As he had prophesied, Mr. Dowsett kept quiet within the room. Listening at the door, I heard him moving softly about, but he made no attempt to come out. At half-past two I entered the room, and followed Devlin's instructions to the letter. Mr. Dowsett, his courage restored, immediately began to bluster and threaten. I listened submissively, and made pretence of being greatly distressed. When he had exhausted himself, I left him with further profuse expressions of regret, and as I issued from the house I saw him mounting the stairs to his wife's apartments.

Emerging into the Rue de la Paix, I planted myself in a spot from which I had a clear view of the house, and was myself concealed from observation. Scarcely was I settled in my position when I saw a man, with a telegram in his hand, enter the house. He remained there a very few moments, and then came out and walked away, having, presumably, delivered his message. Within a space of five minutes, Mr. Dowsett, holding the telegram, came forth, and, casting sharp glances around, quickly left the Rue de la Paix. Before he had turned the corner, Devlin joined me, humming a French song. Together we followed Mr. Dowsett at a safe distance.

"My scheme is alive," he said.

I asked him to explain it to me.

"You saw the messenger," he said, "enter with a telegram. You saw him leave without it. You saw Mr. Dowsett come out with the telegram. It was from his wife."

"From his wife?"

"Sent by me. The telegram was to the effect that something had occurred which had induced her to leave Boulogne immediately, and that she, her daughter, and the young lady with them (I was careful not to mention her name, you see) would be in Ramsgate, waiting for him. He was to come by the afternoon boat, and she would meet him on the pier. See, he is entering the shipping-office now, to secure his passage."

"What are we to do?"

"We travel in the same boat, going aboard at the last moment. After the boat has started – not before – he will know that we are fellow-passengers."

All happened as Devlin had arranged. By his skilful pioneering we did not lose sight of Mr. Dowsett until he stepped aboard the boat, and I inferred from his manner that by that time he had regained confidence, and deemed his secret safe. When we slipped on deck, at the very moment of starting, Mr. Dowsett was below in the saloon.

There were not many passengers, and the French coast was still in view when Mr. Dowsett came up from the saloon and stood by the bulwarks, within a yard or two of the seat upon which we were sitting. We did not speak, but sat watching him. Turning, he saw us.

"You here!" he cried.

"By your leave," I replied.

"Not by my leave," he said. "Why are you following me?"

"Have you any reason," I said, "for suspecting that you are being followed?"

"I was a fool to ask the question," he said, turning abruptly away.

I did not speak, but kept my eyes upon him. I was determined not to lose sight of him for another moment. Some understanding of this determination seemed to dawn upon him; he looked at me two or three times with wavering eyes, and presently, summoning all his courage to his aid, he stared me full in the face. I met his gaze sternly, unflinchingly, until I compelled him to lower his eyes. Then he suddenly went down into the saloon. I stepped swiftly after him, and Devlin accompanied me. For the purpose of testing me, he turned and ascended again to the deck. We followed him.

"Perhaps," he said, "you will explain what you mean by this conduct?"

"What need to ask?" I replied. "Let your conscience answer."

"It is an outrage," he said, after a pause. "If you continue to annoy me, I shall appeal to the captain."

"Do so," I said, "and prepare to meet at once the charge I shall bring against you."

He did not dare to inquire the nature of the charge. He did not dare to move or speak again. Sullenly, and with an inward raging, the traces of which he could not disguise, he remained by the bulwarks, staring down at the water.

Suddenly there was a lull aboard. The machinery stopped working.

"Some accident," said Devlin, and went to ascertain its nature. Returning, he said, "We shall be delayed a couple of hours, most likely. It will be dark night, when we arrive."

It was as he said. For two hours or more we made no progress; then, the necessary repairs having been made, we started again. By that time it was evening. And still Mr. Dowsett neither moved or spoke.

Night crept on; there was no moon, and not a star visible in the dark sky; it was black night. Mr. Dowsett strove to take advantage of this to evade and escape from us, but we kept so close to him that we could have touched him by the movement of a finger; where he glided, we glided; and still he uttered not a word.

We stood in a group alone, isolated as it were, from the other passengers. After repeated attempts to slip from us, Mr. Dowsett remained still again. In the midst of the darkness Devlin's voice stole upon our ears.

"Shortsighted fool," he said, "to think that crime can be for ever successfully hidden. Wherever man moves, the spirit of committed evil accompanies him, and leads him to his doom. His peril lies not only in mortal insight, but in the unseen, mysterious agencies, by which he is surrounded. Blood for blood; it is the immutable law; and if by some human failure he for a time evades his punishment at the hand of man, he suffers a punishment more terrible than human justice can execute upon him. Waking or sleeping, it is ever with him. Look out upon the darkness, and behold, rising from the shadows, the form of the innocent girl whose life you took. To the last moment of your life her spirit shall accompany you; till death claims you, you shall know no peace!"

Whatever of malignancy there was in Devlin's voice, the words he spoke conveyed the stern, eternal truth. It seemed to me, as I gazed before me, that the spirit he evoked loomed sadly among the shadows.

Onward through the sea the boat ploughed its way, and we three stood close together, encompassed by a dread and awful silence; for Devlin spoke no more, nor from Mr. Dowsett's lips did any sound issue.

In the distance we saw the lights of Ramsgate Pier, and before the captain or any person on board was aware of its close contiguity, we suddenly dashed against it.

I and all others on board were thrown violently down by the shock. There were loud cries of alarm and agony, and I found myself separated from my companions. From the water came appeals for help from some who had been tossed overboard by the collision, and a period of great confusion ensued. What help could be given was afforded, and when I succeeded in reaching the stone pier in safety, I heard that a few of the passengers were missing – among them Devlin and Mr. Dowsett.

I remained on the pier till past one o'clock in the morning, rendering what little assistance I could; and eventually I learnt that all who had been in danger were saved, with the exception of the two whom I have named. It was early morning before the body of one was recovered. That one was Mr. Kenneth Dowsett. He lay dead in a boat, his face convulsed with agony, upturned to the gray light of the coming day. Of Devlin no trace could be found.

* * *

There is but little more to tell. With the exception of the part which Devlin played in it, and which has now for the first time been related, the story became public property, and Kenneth Dowsett was proved to be the murderer of poor

Mary Melladew. Time has softened the grief of Mr. and Mrs. Melladew, and they find in the love of Lizzie and her husband, Richard Carton, some solace for the tragedy which a ruthless hand committed. Mr. Portland paid me the two thousand pounds he promised, and I am in a fair way of business. Fanny Lemon and her husband live in retirement in the country. Not a word ever passes their lips in connection with the events I have related. I have seen and heard nothing of Mrs. Dowsett and her daughter.

* * *

A short time ago my wife and I were in an open-air public place of amusement witnessing a wonderful exhibition, the extraordinary novelty of which consisted in a man floating earthwards from the clouds at a distance of some thousands of feet from the earth.

"Look there!" said my wife.

I had given her such faithful and vivid descriptions of Devlin that she always said, if it happened that he still lived and she saw him, that she could not fail to recognise him. I turned in the direction she indicated, and, standing alone, apart from the crowd, once more saw Devlin. He was watching the performer floating from heaven to earth. There was a strange smile upon his lips.

I could not restrain the impulse which prompted me to move towards him. My approach attracted his attention. He looked at me, and was gone. I have never seen him since.

The last words I heard him speak recur to me. There was in them the spirit of Divine justice. Crimes cannot be forever successfully hidden. The monsters who commit them shall be brought to their doom by those whose duty it is to track them down, or by unseen mysterious agencies by which they are surrounded, or by their own confession.

But let the legislators see to it; let those who call themselves philanthropists and humanitarians see to it; let those whose fortune it is to possess great wealth see to it. There are in this modern Babylon fester-spots of corruption wherein nothing but sin and vice can possibly grow. They are crowded with human beings ripening for evil; they are crowded with human souls lost to salvation. They are an infamy – and the infamy rests not upon the creatures who are born and bred there, but upon those who allow them to be, and who have the undoubted power to cleanse them, and make them healthy for body and soul. For generation upon generation have they been allowed to breed corruption; to this day they are allowed to do so. All who have the remedy in their hands are responsible. The preacher who preaches and does not practise; the rich who can afford, but grudges to give; the statesman with his dilettante efforts towards social improvement, and his huge efforts towards place and power – one and all of these are accountable for the sin. It is no less, and it rests upon them.

THE END